The Mozart Question

Michael Morpurgo

Illustrated by

Michael Foreman

WALKER
BOOKS

For Christine Baker – M. M. & M. F.

The question I am most often asked is always easy enough to answer. Question: how did you get started as a writer? Answer: funnily enough, by asking someone almost exactly that very same question, which I was only able to ask in the first place by a dose of extraordinarily good fortune.

I had better explain.

My good fortune was, of course, someone else's rotten luck – it is often that way, I find. The phone call sounded distraught. It came on a Sunday evening. I had only been working on the paper for three weeks. I was a cub reporter, this my first paid job.

"Lesley?" It was my boss, chief arts correspondent Meryl Monkton, a lady not to be messed with. She did not waste time with niceties; she never did. "Listen, Lesley, I have a problem. I was due to go to Venice tomorrow to interview Paolo Levi."

"Paolo Levi?" I said. "The violinist?"

"Is there any other Paolo Levi?" She did not trouble to hide her irritation. "Now look, Lesley. I've had an accident, a skiing accident, and I'm stuck in hospital in Switzerland. You'll have to go to Venice instead of me."

"Oh, that's terrible," I said, smothering as best I could the excitement surging inside me. Three weeks into the job and I'd be interviewing the great Paolo Levi, and in Venice!

Talk about her accident, I told myself. Sound concerned. Sound very concerned.

"How did it happen?" I asked. "The skiing accident, I mean."

"Skiing," she snapped. "If there's one thing I can't abide, Lesley, it's people feeling sorry for me."

"Sorry," I said.

"I would postpone it if I could, Lesley," she went on, "but I just don't dare. It's taken me more than a year to persuade him to do it. It'll be his first interview in years. And even then I had to agree not to ask him the Mozart question. So don't ask him the Mozart question, is that clear? If you do he'll like as not cancel the whole interview – he's done it before. We're really lucky to get him, Lesley. I only wish I could be there to do it myself. But you'll have to do."

"The Mozart question?" I asked, rather tentatively.

The silence at the end of the phone was long.

"You mean to say you don't know about Paolo Levi and the Mozart question? Where have you been, girl? Don't you know anything at all about Paolo Levi?"

I suddenly felt I might lose the opportunity altogether if I did not immediately sound informed, and well informed too.

"Well, he would have been born sometime in the mid-1950s," I began. "He must be about fifty by now."

"Exactly fifty in two weeks' time," Meryl Monkton interrupted wearily. "His London concert is his fiftieth birthday concert. That's the whole point of the interview. Go on."

I rattled off all I knew. "Child prodigy and genius, like Yehudi Menuhin. Played his first major concert when he was thirteen. Probably best known for his playing of Bach and Vivaldi. Like Menuhin he played often with Grappelli, equally at home with jazz or Scottish fiddle music or Beethoven. Has played in practically every major concert hall in the world, in front of presidents and kings and queens. I heard him at the Royal Festival Hall in London, five years ago, I think. He was playing Beethoven's Violin Concerto; he was wonderful. Doesn't like applause. Never waits for

applause. Doesn't believe in it, apparently. The night I saw him he just walked off the stage and didn't come back. He thinks it's the music that should be applauded if anything, or perhaps the composer, but certainly not the musician. Says that the silence after the performance is part of the music and should not be interrupted. Doesn't record either.

Believes music should be live, not canned. Protects his privacy fiercely. Solitary. Reticent. Lives alone in Venice, where he was born. Just about the most famous musician on the planet, and—"

"*The* most famous, Lesley, but he hates obsequiousness. He likes to be talked to straight. So no bowing or scraping, no wide-eyed wonder, and above all no nerves. Can you do that?"

"Yes, Meryl," I replied, knowing only too well that I would have the greatest difficulty even finding my voice in front of the great man.

"And whatever you do, stick to the music. He'll talk till the cows come home about music and composers. But no personal stuff. And above all, keep off the Mozart question. Oh yes, and don't take a tape recorder with you. He hates gadgets. Only shorthand. You can do shorthand, I suppose? Three thousand words. It's your big chance, so don't mess it up, Lesley."

No pressure, then, I thought.

❊   ❊   ❊

So there I was the next evening outside Paolo Levi's apartment in the Dorsoduro in Venice, on the dot of six o'clock, my throat dry, my heart pounding, trying all I could to compose myself. It occurred to me again, as it had often on the plane, that I still had no idea what this Mozart question was, only that I mustn't ask it. It was cold, the kind of cruel chill that seeps instantly into your bones, deep into your kidneys, and makes your ears ache. This didn't seem to bother the street performers in the square behind me: several grotesquely masked figures on stilts strutting across the square, an entirely silver statue-man posing immobile outside the café with a gaggle of tourists gazing wonderingly at him.

The door opened, and there he was in front of me, Paolo Levi, neat, trim, his famous hair long to his shoulders and jet black.

"I'm Lesley McInley," I said. "I've come from London."

"From the newspaper, I suppose." There was no welcoming smile. "You'd better come in. Shut the door behind you; I hate the cold." His English was perfect, not a trace of an accent. He seemed to be able to follow my thoughts. "I speak English quite well," he said as we went up the stairs. "Language is like music. You learn it best through listening."

He led me down a hallway and into a large room, empty except for a couch by the window piled high with cushions at one end, a grand piano in the centre and a music stand near by. At the other end were just two armchairs and a table. Nothing else. "I like to keep it empty," he said.

It was uncanny. He *was* reading my thoughts. Now I felt even more unnerved.

"Sound needs space to breathe, just the same as we need air," he said.

He waved me to a chair and sat down. "You'll have some

mint tea?" he said, pouring me a cup. His dark blue cardigan and grey corduroy trousers were somehow both shabby and elegant at the same time. The bedroom slippers he wore looked incongruous but comfortable. "My feet, they hate the cold more than the rest of me." He was scrutinizing me

now, his eyes sharp and shining. "You're younger than I expected," he said. "Twenty-three?" He didn't wait to have his estimate confirmed – he knew he was right and he was. "You have heard me play?"

"Beethoven's Violin Concerto. The Royal Festival Hall in London, a few years ago. I was a student." I noticed his violin then, and his bow, on the window ledge.

"I like to practise by the window," he said, "so I can watch the world go by on the canal. It passes the time. Even as a child I never liked practising much. And I love to be near water, to look out on it. When I go to London I have to have a room by the Thames. In Paris I must be by the Seine. I love the light that water makes." He sipped his mint tea, his eyes never leaving me. "Shouldn't you be asking me questions?" He went on. "I'm talking too much. Journalists always make me nervous. I talk too much when I'm nervous. When I go to the dentist's I talk. Before a concert I talk. So let's get this over with, shall we? And not too many questions, please. Why don't we keep it simple? You ask me one question and then let me ramble on. Shall we try that?" I didn't feel at all that he was being dismissive or patronizing, just straight. That didn't make it any easier, though.

I had done my research, made pages of notes, prepared dozens of questions; but now, under his expectant gaze, I simply could not gather my thoughts.

"Well, I know I can't ask you the Mozart question, Signor Levi," I began, "because I've been told not to. I don't even know what the Mozart question is, so I couldn't ask it even if I wanted to; and anyway, I know you don't like it, so I won't."

With every blundering word I was digging myself into a deeper hole. In my desperation I blurted out the first question that came into my head.

"Signor Levi," I said, "I wonder if you'd mind telling me how you got started. I mean, what made you pick up a violin and play that first time?" It was such an obvious question, and personal too, just the kind of question I shouldn't have asked.

His reaction only confirmed that. He sat back in his chair and closed his eyes. For fully a couple of minutes he said nothing. I was quite sure he was trying to control his impatience, his rage even, that he was going to open his eyes and ask me to leave at once. When he did open his eyes he simply stared up at the ceiling for a while. I could see from the seriousness of his whole demeanour that he was making a decision, and I feared the worst. But instead of throwing me out he stood up and walked slowly to the couch by the window. He picked up his violin and sat back on the cushions with his violin resting on his drawn-up knees. He plucked a string or two and tuned it.

"I will tell you a story," he began. "After it is over you will need to ask me no more questions. Someone once told me that all secrets are lies. The time has come, I think, not to lie any more."

He paused. I felt he was stiffening his resolve, gathering his strength.

"I will start with my father. Papa was a barber. He kept a little barber's shop just behind the Accademia, near the bridge, two minutes from here. We lived above the shop, Mama, Papa and I, but I spent most of my time downstairs in the barber's shop, sitting on the chairs and swinging my legs, smiling at him and his customers in the mirror, and just watching him. I loved those days. I loved him. At the time of these memories I must have been about nine years old. Small for my age. I always was. I still am."

He spoke slowly, very deliberately, as if he was living it again, seeing again everything he was telling me. My shorthand was quick and automatic, so I had time to look up at him occasionally as he spoke. I sensed right away that I was the first person ever to hear this story, so I knew even as he told it just how momentous the telling of it was for him, as in a totally different way it was for me too.

"Papa was infinitely deft with his fingers, his scissors playing a constantly changing tune. It seemed to me like a new improvisation for every customer, the snipping unhesitatingly skilful, so fast it was mesmerizing. He would work always in complete silence, conducting the music of his scissors with his comb. His customers knew better than to interrupt the performance, and so did I. I think perhaps I must have known his customers almost as well as he did. I grew up with them. They were all regulars. Some would close their eyes as Papa worked his magic; others would look back in the mirror at me and wink.

"Shaving was just as fascinating to me, just as rhythmical too: the swift sweep and dab of the brush, the swish and slap of the razor as Papa sharpened it on the strap, then each time the miraculous unmasking as he stroked the foam away to reveal a recognizable face once more.

"After it was all over, he and his customers did talk, and all the banter amongst them was about football, Inter Milan in particular, or sometimes the machinations of politicians and women. What they said I cannot exactly remember, probably because I couldn't understand most of it, but I do know they

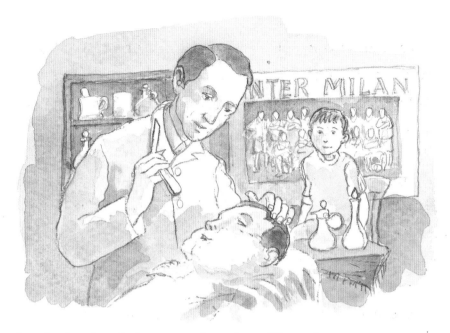

laughed a lot. I do remember that. Then the next customer would take his seat and a new silence would descend before the performance started and the music of the scissors began. I am sure I first learnt about rhythm in that barber's shop, and about concentration. I learnt to listen too.

"Papa wasn't just the best barber in all of Venice – everyone said that – he was a musician too, a violinist. But strangely he was a violinist who never played the violin. I never heard him play, not once. I only knew he was a violinist because Mama had told me so. She had tears in her eyes whenever she told me about it. That surprised me because she was not a crying woman. He had been so brilliant as a violinist, the best in the whole orchestra, she said. When I asked why he didn't play any more, she turned away from me, went very quiet and told me I'd have to ask Papa myself. So I did. I asked him time and again, and each time he would simply shrug, and say something meaningless like: 'People change, Paolo. Times change.' And that would be that.

"Papa was never a great talker at the best of times, even at home, but I could tell that in this case he was hiding something, that he found my questions both irksome and intrusive. That didn't stop me. I kept on at him. Every time he refused to talk about it I became more suspicious, more sure he had something to hide. It was a child's intuition, I suppose. I sensed a deep secret, but I also sensed after a while that Papa was quite unmovable, that if I was ever going to unlock the secret it would be Mama who would tell me.

"As it turned out, my instinct was right. In the end my almost perpetual pestering proved fruitful, and Mama capitulated

– but not in a way I had expected. 'All right, Paolo,' she said after I'd been nagging her about it unmercifully one morning. 'If I show you the violin will you promise me you'll stop asking your wretched questions? And you're never ever to tell Papa I showed you. He'd be very angry. Promise me now.'

"So I promised, promised faithfully, and then stood in their bedroom and watched as she climbed up on a chair to get it down from where it had been hidden on top of the cupboard. It was wrapped up in an old grey blanket. I knelt on the bed beside her as she pulled away the blanket and opened the violin case. I remember it smelt musty. The maroon lining inside was faded and worn to tatters. Mama picked up the violin with infinite care, reverently almost. Then she handed it to me.

"I stroked the polished grain of the wood, which was the colour of honey, dark honey on the front, and golden honey underneath. I ran my fingers along the black pegs, the mottled bridge, the exquisitely carved scroll. It was so light to hold, I remember. I wondered at its fragile beauty. I knew at once that all the music in the world was hidden away inside this violin, yearning to come out. I longed to be the one to let it out, to rest it under my chin, to play the strings, to try the bow. I wanted there and then to bring it to life, to have it sing for me, to hear all the music we could make together. But when I asked if I could play it, Mama took sudden fright and said Papa might hear down below in the barber's shop, and he'd be furious with her for showing it to me; that he never wanted it to be played again. He hadn't so much as looked at it in years. When I asked why, she reminded me of my promise not to ask any more questions. She almost snatched the violin off me, laid it back in its case, wrapped it again in the blanket and put it back up on top of the cupboard.

"'You don't know it exists, Paolo. You never saw it, understand? And from now on I don't want to hear another word about it, all right? You promised me, Paolo.'

"I suppose seeing Papa's old violin, holding it as I had,

marvelling at it, must have satisfied my curiosity for a while, because I kept my promise. Then late one summer's evening I was lying half awake in my bed when I heard the sound of a violin. I thought Papa must have changed his mind and was playing again at last. But then I heard him and Mama talking in the kitchen below, and realized anyway that the music was coming from much further away.

"I listened at the window. I could hear it only intermittently over the sound of people talking and walking, over the throbbing engines of passing water buses, but I was quite sure now that it was coming from somewhere beyond the bridge. I had to find out. In my pyjamas I stole past the kitchen door, down the stairs and out into the street. It was a warm night, and quite dark. I ran up over the bridge and there, all on his own, standing by the lamp in the square, was an old man playing the violin, his violin case open at his feet.

"No one else was there. No one had stopped to listen. I squatted down as close as I dared. He was so wrapped up in his playing that he did not notice me at first. I could see now that he was much older even than Papa. Then he saw me crouching there watching him. He stopped playing. 'Hello,' he said. 'You're out late. What's your name?' He had kind eyes; I noticed that at once.

"'Paolo,' I told him. 'Paolo Levi. My papa plays the violin. He played in an orchestra once.'

"'So did I,' said the old man, 'all my life. But now I am what I always wanted to be, a soloist. I shall play you some Mozart. Do you like Mozart?'

"'I don't know,' I replied. I knew Mozart's name, of course, but I don't think I had ever listened to any of his music.

"'He wrote this piece when he was even younger than you. I should guess that you're about seven.'

"'Nine,' I said.

"'Well, Mozart wrote this when he was just six years old. He wrote it for the piano, but I can play it on the violin.'

"So he played Mozart, and I listened. As he played, others

came and gathered round for a while before dropping a coin or two in his violin case and moving on. I didn't move on. I stayed. The music he played to me that night touched my soul. It was the night that changed my life for ever.

"Whenever I crossed the Accademia Bridge after that I always looked out for him. Whenever I heard him playing I went to listen. I never told Mama or Papa. I think it was the first secret I kept from them. But I did not feel guilty about it, not one bit. After all, hadn't they kept a secret from me? Then one evening the old man – I had found out by now that his name was Benjamin Horowitz and that he was sixty-two years old – one evening he let me hold his violin, showed me how to hold it properly, how to draw the bow across the strings, how to make it sing. The moment I did that, I knew I had to be a violinist. I have never wanted to do or be anything else since.

"So Benjamin – Signor Horowitz I always called him then – became my first teacher. Now every time I ran over the bridge to see him he would show me a little more, how to tighten the bow just right, how to use the resin, how to hold the violin under my chin using no hands at all and what each string was called. That was when I told him about Papa's violin at home, and about how he didn't play it any more. 'He couldn't anyway,' I said, 'because it's a bit broken. I think it needs mending a bit. Two of the strings are missing, the A and the E, and there's hardly a hair left on the bow at all. But I could practise on it if it was mended, couldn't I?'

"'Bring it to my house sometime,' Benjamin said, 'and leave it with me. I'll see what I can do.'

"It wasn't difficult to escape unnoticed. I just waited till after school. Mama was still at the laundry round the corner in Rio de le Romite where she worked. Papa was downstairs with his customers. To reach the violin on top of the cupboard I had to put a suitcase on the chair and then climb up. It wasn't easy but I managed. I ran through the streets hugging it to me.

From the Dorsoduro to the Arsenale where Benjamin lived is not that far if you know the way – nowhere is that far in Venice – and I knew the way quite well because my Aunt Sophia lived there and we visited her often. All I had to do was find Benjamin's street. I had to ask about a bit, but I found it.

"Benjamin lived up a narrow flight of stairs in one small room with a bed in one corner and a basin in the other. On the wall were lots of concert posters. 'Some of the concerts I played,' he said. 'Milan, London, New York. Wonderful places, wonderful people, wonderful music. It is a wonderful world out there. There are times when it can be hard to go on believing that. But always believe it, Paolo, because it is true. And music helps to make it so. Now, show me that violin of yours.'

"He studied it closely, holding it up to the light, tapping it. 'A very fine instrument,' he said. 'You say this belongs to your father?'

"'And now I want to play it myself,' I told him.

"'It's a bit on the large side for a young lad like you,' he said, tucking the violin under my chin and stretching my arm to see

how far I could reach. 'But a big violin is better than no violin at all. You'll manage. You'll grow into it.'

"'And when it's mended, will you teach me?' I asked him. 'I've got lots of money saved up from my sweeping; so many notes they cover all my bed when I spread them out, from the end of the bed right up to my pillow.'

"He laughed at that and told me he would teach me for nothing because I was his best listener, his lucky mascot. 'When you're not there,' he said, 'everyone walks by and my violin case stays empty. Then you come along and sit there.

That's when they always stop to listen and that's when they leave their money. So a lesson or two will just be paying you back, Paolo. I'll have the violin ready as soon as I can and then we can start your lessons.'

"It was a week or two before the violin was mended. I dreaded that Mama or Papa might discover it was missing. But my luck held, and they didn't, and my

lessons began. Whenever I wasn't having my lessons with Benjamin, Papa's violin, now restrung and restored, lay in its case wrapped in the grey blanket and hidden away on top of their bedroom cupboard. My secret was safe, I thought. But secrets are never safe, however well hidden. Sooner or later truth will out, and in this case it was to be sooner rather than later.

"I took to the violin as if it had

been a limb I had been missing all my life. I seemed to be able to pick up everything Benjamin taught me, effortlessly and instinctively. Under his kind tutelage my confidence simply burgeoned, my playing blossomed. I found I could make my violin – Papa's violin rather – sing with the voice of an angel. Benjamin and I felt the excitement and pleasure of my progress as keenly as each other. 'I think this instrument was invented just for you, Paolo,' he told me one day. 'Or maybe you were made for it. Either way it is a perfect match.' I loved every precious moment of my lessons and always dreaded their ending. We would finish every lesson with a cup of mint tea made with fresh mint. I loved it. Ever since, I have always treated myself to a cup of mint tea after practice. It's something I always look forward to.

"I remember one day with the lesson over, we were drinking tea at his table when he looked across at me, suddenly very serious. 'It is strange, Paolo,' he said, 'but as I was watching you playing a moment ago, I felt I had known you before, a long, long time ago. And then just now I thought about your name, Levi. It is a common enough name, I know, but

his name was Levi too. It is him you remind me of. I am sure of it. He was the youngest player in our orchestra, no more than a boy really. Gino, he was called.'

"'But my father is called Gino,' I told him. 'Maybe it was him. Maybe you played with my father. Maybe you know him.'

"'It can't be possible,' Benjamin breathed. He was staring at me now as if I were a ghost. 'No, it can't be. The Gino Levi I knew must be dead, I am sure of it. I have not heard of him in a long while, a very long while. But you never know, I suppose. Maybe I should meet your papa, and your mama too. It's about time anyway. You've been coming for lessons for over six months now. They need to know they have a wonderful violinist for a son.'

"'No, you can't!' I cried. 'He'd find out! You can't tell him. You mustn't!' Then I told him, through my tears, all my secret, about how Mama had shown me Papa's violin and made me promise never to say anything, never to tell Papa, and how I'd kept it a secret all this while, mending the violin, the lessons, everything.

"'Secrets, Paolo,' said Benjamin, 'are lies by another name. You do not lie to those you love. A son should not hide things from his papa and his mama. You must tell them your secret, Paolo. If you want to go on playing the violin, you will have to tell them. If you want me to go on teaching you, you will have to tell them. And now is usually a good time to do what must be done, particularly when you don't want to do it.'

"'Will you come with me?' I begged him. 'I can only do it if you come with me.'

"'If you like,' he said, smiling.

"Benjamin carried Papa's violin for me that day, and held my hand all the way back to the Dorsoduro. I dreaded having to make my confession. I knew how hurt they would be. All the way I rehearsed what I was going to say over and over again.

Mama and Papa were upstairs in the kitchen when we came in. I introduced Benjamin and then, before anyone had a chance to say anything, before I lost my courage entirely, I launched at once into my prepared confession, how I hadn't really stolen Papa's violin, just borrowed it to get it mended, and to practise on. But that's as far as I got. To my surprise they were not looking angry. In fact, they weren't looking at me at all. They were just staring up at Benjamin as if quite unable to speak. Benjamin spoke before they did. 'Your mama and papa and me, I think perhaps we do know one another,' he said. 'We played together once, did we not? Don't you remember me, Gino?'

"'Benjamin?' As Papa started to his feet, the chair went over behind him.

"'And if I am not much mistaken, Signora,' Benjamin went on, looking now at Mama, 'you must be little Laura Adler – all of us violins, all of us there, and all of us still here. It is like a miracle. It *is* a miracle.'

"What happened next I can see as if it were yesterday. It was suddenly as if I was not in the room at all. The three of them seemed to fill the kitchen, arms around each other,

and crying openly, crying through their laughter. I stood there mystified, trying to piece together all I had heard, all that was going on before my eyes. Mama played the violin too! She had never told me that!

"'You see, Paolo,' said Benjamin, smiling down at me, 'didn't I tell you once it was a wonderful world? Twenty years. It's been twenty years or more since I last saw your mama and papa. I had no idea they were still alive. I always hoped they survived, hoped they were together, these two young love-birds, but I never believed it, not really.'

"Mama was drying her eyes on her apron. Papa was so overcome, he couldn't speak. They sat down then, hands joined around the table as if unwilling to let each other go for fear this reunion might turn out to be no more than a dream.

"Benjamin was the first to recover. 'Paolo was about to tell you something, I think,' he said. 'Weren't you, Paolo?' I told them everything then: how I'd gone for my lessons, how Benjamin had been the best teacher in all the world. I dared to look up only when I'd finished. Instead of the disapproval and disappointment I had expected, both Mama and Papa were simply glowing with joy and pride.

"'Didn't I say Paolo would tell us, Papa?' she said. 'Didn't I tell you we should trust him? You see, Paolo, I often take down my violin, just to touch it, to look at it. Papa doesn't like me to, but I do it all the same, because this violin is my oldest friend. Papa forgives me, because he knows I love this violin, that it is a part of me. You remember I showed it to you that day, Paolo? It wasn't long after that it went missing, was it? I knew it had to be you. Then it came back, mended miraculously. And after school you were never home, and when you weren't home the violin was always gone too. I told Papa, didn't I, Papa? I told him you'd tell us when you were ready. We put two and two together; we thought you might be practising somewhere, but it never occurred to us that you were having lessons, nor that you had a teacher – and certainly not that your teacher was Benjamin Horowitz, who taught us and looked after us like a father all those years ago.' She cried again then, her head on Papa's shoulder.

"'But you told me it was Papa's violin, that he'd put it away and never wanted to play it again, ever,' I said.

"At this the three of them looked at one another. I knew then they all shared the same secret, and that without a word passing between them they were deciding whether they should reveal it, if this was the right moment to tell me. I often wondered later whether, if Benjamin had not come that day, they would ever have told me. As it was they looked to Papa for the final decision, and it was he who invited me to the table to join them. I think I knew then, even before Papa began, that I was in some way part of their secret.

"'Mama and me,' Papa began, 'we try never to speak of this, because the memories we have are like nightmares, and we want to forget. But you told us your secret. There is a time for truth, it seems, and it has come. Truth for truth, maybe.'

"So began the saddest, yet the happiest story I ever heard. When the story became too painful, as it often did, they passed it from one to the other, so that all three shared it. I listened horrified, at the same time honoured that they trusted me enough with their story, the story of their lives. Each told their part with great care, explaining as they went along so that I would understand, because I was a boy of nine who knew very little then of the wickedness of the world. I wish I could remember their exact words, but I can't, so I won't even try. I'll just tell you their story my own way, about how they lived together, how they nearly died together and how they were saved by music.

"The three of them were brought by train to the concentration camp from all over Europe: Benjamin from Paris, Mama from Warsaw, Papa from here, from Venice; all musicians, all Jewish, and all bound for the gas chamber and extermination like so many millions. They survived only because they were all able to say yes to one question put to them by an SS officer on arrival at the camp. 'Is there anyone amongst you who can play an orchestral instrument, who is a professional musician?' They did not know when they stepped forward that they would at once be separated from their families, would have to watch them being herded off towards those hellish chimneys, never to be seen again.

"There were auditions, of course, and by now they knew they were playing for their lives. There were rehearsals then, and it was during these rehearsals that the three of them first met. Benjamin was a good twenty years older than Mama and Papa, who were very much the babies of the orchestra, both of them just twenty. Why the orchestra was rehearsing, who they would be playing for, they did not know and they did not ask. To ask was to draw attention to oneself. This they knew was not the way to survive, and in the camp to survive was everything. They played Mozart, a lot of Mozart. The repertoire was for the most part light and happy – *Eine kleine Nachtmusick*, the Clarinet Concerto in A major, minuets, dances, marches. And Strauss was popular too, waltzes, always waltzes. Playing was very hard because their fingers were so cold that sometimes they could hardly feel them, because they were weak with hunger and frequently sick. Sickness had to be hidden, because sickness once discovered would mean death. The SS were always there watching, and everyone knew too what awaited them if they did not play well enough.

"At first they gave concerts only for the SS officers. Papa said you just had to pretend they were not there. You simply lost yourself in the music – it was the only way. Even when they applauded you did not look up. You never looked them in the eye. You played with total commitment. Every performance was your best performance, not to please them, but to show them what you could do, to prove to them how good you

were despite all they were doing to humiliate you, to destroy you in body and soul. 'We fought back with our music,' Papa said. 'It was our only weapon.'

"Papa could speak no Polish, Mama no Italian, but their eyes met as they were playing – as often as possible, Mama said. To begin with, it might have been their shared joy in music-making, but very soon they knew they loved one another. The whole orchestra knew it, even before they did, Benjamin told me. 'Our little lovebirds' they were called. For everyone else in the orchestra, he said, they represented a symbol of hope for the future; and so they were much loved, much protected. For Mama and Papa their love numbed the pain and was a blessed refuge from the constant fear they were living through, from the horror of all that was going on around them.

"But there was amongst them a shared shame. They were being fed when others were not. They were being kept alive while others went to the gas chamber. Many were consumed by guilt, and this guilt was multiplied a thousand times when they discovered the real reason the orchestra had been assembled, why they had been rehearsing all this time. The concerts for the SS officers turned out to be sinister dress rehearsals for something a great deal worse.

"One cold morning with snow on the ground, they were made to assemble out in the compound with their instruments and ordered to sit down and play close to the camp gates. Then the train arrived, the wagons packed with new prisoners.

Once they were all out they were lined up and then divided. The old and young and the frail were herded past the orchestra on their way, they were told, to the shower block; the able-bodied, those fit for work, were taken off towards the huts. And all the while Mama and Papa and Benjamin and the others played their Mozart. They all understood soon enough what it was for – to calm the terror, to beguile each new trainload into a false sense of security. They were part of a deadly sham. They knew well enough that the shower block was a gas chamber.

"Week after week they played, month after month, train after train. And twenty-four hours a day the chimneys of the crematorium spewed out their fire and their smoke and their stench. Until there were no more trains; until the day the camps were liberated. This was the last day Benjamin ever remembered seeing Mama and Papa. They were all terribly emaciated by now, he said, and looked unlikely to survive. But they had. Mama and Papa had walked together out of the camp. They had played duets for bread and shelter, all across Europe. They were still playing to survive.

"When at last they got home to Venice, Papa smashed his violin and burned it, vowing never to play music again. But Mama kept hers. She thought of it as her talisman, her saviour and her friend, and she would neither sell it nor abandon it. She said it had brought her through all the horrors of the camp, brought them safely across Europe, back to Papa's home in Venice. It had saved their lives.

"Papa kept his vow. He never played a note of music again. After all that had happened he could hardly bear to hear it, which is why Mama had not played her violin either in all these years. But she would not be parted from it and had kept it safe at the top of their bedroom cupboard, hoping against hope, she said, that one day Papa might change his mind and be able to love music again and even play it. He never had. But they had survived and they were in time blessed with a child, a boy they called Paolo – a happy ending, Benjamin said. And I was the one who had brought the three of them together again, he said. So two happy endings.

"As for Benjamin, he had found his way back to Paris after a while, and played again in his old orchestra. He had married a French girl, Françoise, a cellist who had died only recently. He had come to Venice because he had always loved visiting the city and always longed to live looking out over water, and because Vivaldi was born here – he had always loved Vivaldi above all other composers. He played in the streets not just for the money, though that was a help, but because he could not bear not to play his violin. And he loved playing solo violin at last. He was more like Mama, he said. It was music that had kept him alive in the camp, and music had been his constant companion ever since. He could not imagine living a single day of his life without it, which was

why, he said, he would dearly like to go on teaching me, if Mama and Papa would allow it.

"'Does he play well, Benjamin?' Mama asked. 'Can we hear him, Papa? Please.'

"Papa, I could see, was struggling with himself. 'So long as it's not Mozart,' he said finally. So I played the Winter movement from Vivaldi's *Four Seasons*, Benjamin's favourite piece. Papa sat listening with closed eyes throughout.

"When I had finished, Benjamin said, 'Well, Gino, what do you think? He has a great and wonderful talent, your son, a rare gift you have both given him.'

"'Then it must not be wasted,' said Papa quietly.

"So every day without fail after that I went for my violin lessons with Benjamin in his little apartment in the Arsenale. Papa could not bring himself to listen to me playing, but sometimes Mama came along with me and sat and listened, and afterwards she always hugged me so tight it hurt; but I did not mind, not one bit. I began to play in the streets alongside Benjamin, and whenever I did the crowds became bigger and bigger each time. One day Papa was there amongst them watching, listening.

He walked me home afterwards, saying not a word until we were walking over the Accademia Bridge. 'So, Paolo,' he said, 'you prefer playing the violin to sweeping up in my barber's shop, do you?'

"'Yes, Papa,' I replied. 'I'm afraid I do.'

"'Well then, I can see I shall just have to do my sweeping up myself.' He stopped then and put his hands on my shoulders. 'I shall tell you something, Paolo, and I want you never to forget it. When you play I can listen to music again. You have made music joyful for me once more, and that is a wonderful gift you have given me. You go and be the great violinist you should be. I shall help you all I can. You will play heavenly music and people will love you. Mama and I shall come to all your concerts, or as many as we can. But you have to promise me one thing: that until the day I die you will never play Mozart in public, not in my hearing. It was Mozart we played so often in the camp. Never Mozart. Promise me.'

"So I promised. I have kept my promise to Papa all these years. He died two weeks ago, the last of the three of them to go.

At my fiftieth birthday concert in London I shall be playing Mozart, and I shall be playing it on Mama's violin, and I shall play it so well that he will love it, they will all love it, wherever they are."

I was still finishing my shorthand when I looked up and saw him coming towards me. He was offering me his violin.

"Here you are," he said. "Mama's violin. My violin. You can hold it if you like while we have some more mint tea. You'll have another cup, won't you? I make the best mint tea in Venice."

So I held Paolo Levi's violin for several precious minutes as we sat talking quietly over a last cup of tea. I asked him no more questions. There were none to ask. He talked of his love of Venice, and how wherever he was in the world he longed to be back home. It was the sounds he always missed: the church bells, the walking and talking, the chuntering of boats, and the music in the streets. "Music belongs in the streets, where Benjamin played it," he said, "not in concert halls."

As I left, he looked me in the eye and said, still grasping my hand, "I am glad it was you I told."

"Why did you?" I asked. "Why did you tell me?"

"Because it was time to tell the truth. Because secrets are lies, and because you have eyes that are kind, like Benjamin's. But mostly because you didn't ask the Mozart question."

Author's Note

It is difficult for us to imagine how dreadful was the suffering that went on in the Nazi concentration camps during the Second World War. The enormity of the crime that the Nazis committed is just too overwhelming for us to comprehend. In their attempt to wipe out an entire race they caused the deaths of six million people, most of them Jews. It is when you hear the stories of the individuals who lived through it – Anne Frank, Primo Levi – that you can begin to understand the horror just a little better, and to understand the evil that caused it.

For me, the most haunting image does not come from literature or film, but from music. I learned some time ago that in many of the camps the Nazis selected Jewish prisoners and forced them to play in orchestras; for the musicians it was simply a way to survive. In order to calm the new arrivals at the camps they were made to serenade them as they were lined up and marched off, many to the gas chambers. Often they played Mozart.

I wondered how it must have been for a musician who played in such hellish circumstances, who adored Mozart as I do – what thoughts came when playing Mozart later in life. This was the genesis of my story, this and the sight of a small boy in a square by the Accademia Bridge in Venice, sitting one night, in his pyjamas on his tricycle, listening to a busker. He sat totally enthralled by the music that seemed to him, and to me, to be heavenly.

Michael Morpurgo

This is a work of fiction.
Names, characters, places and incidents are either the product of the author's imagination or, if real, are used fictitiously.
First published 2006 in *Singing for Mrs Pettigrew: A Story-maker's Journey* by Walker Books Ltd, 87 Vauxhall Walk, London SE11 5HJ
This edition published 2008
4 6 8 10 9 7 5
Text © 2006 Michael Morpurgo Illustrations © 2007 Michael Foreman
The right of Michael Morpurgo and Michael Foreman to be identified as author and illustrator respectively of this work
has been asserted by them in accordance with the Copyright, Designs and Patents Act 1988
This book has been typeset in Bodoni
Printed in China

British Library Cataloguing in Publication Data: a catalogue record for this book is available from the British Library
ISBN 978-1-4063-1220-1
www.walker.co.uk

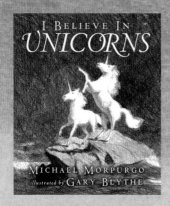

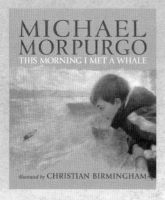

This Morning
I Met a Whale

First published 2008 by Walker Books Ltd
87 Vauxhall Walk, London SE11 5HJ

This edition published 2009

4 6 8 10 9 7 5

Text © 2008 Michael Morpurgo
Illustrations © 2008 Christian Birmingham

This book has been typeset in ITC Giovanni

Printed in China

British Library Cataloguing in Publication Data:
a catalogue record for this book is available from the British Library

ISBN 978-1-4063-1559-2

www.walker.co.uk

This Morning
I Met a Whale

Michael Morpurgo

illustrated by

Christian Birmingham

WALKER
BOOKS

T his morning I met a whale. It was just after five o'clock and I was down by the river. Sometimes, when my alarm clock works, and when I feel like it, I get up early, because I like to go bird-watching, because bird-watching is my favourite hobby. I usually go just before first light. Mum doesn't mind, just so long as I don't wake her up, just so long as I'm back for breakfast.

It's the best time. You get to hear the dawn chorus. You get to see the sunrise and the whole world waking up around you. That's when the birds come flying down to the river to feed, and I can watch them landing in the water. I love that.

5

If you're already there when they come, they hardly notice you, and then you don't bother them. Hardly anyone else is down by the river at five o'clock, sometimes no one at all, just the birds and me. The rest of London is asleep. Well, mostly anyway.

From our flat in Battersea it takes about five minutes to walk down to the river. The first bird I saw this morning was a heron. I love herons because they stand so still in the shallows. They're looking for fish, waiting to strike. When they strike they do it so fast, it's like lightning, and when they catch something they look so surprised and so pleased with themselves, as if they've never done it before. When they walk they walk in slow motion. When they take off and fly they look prehistoric, like pteradactyls almost. Herons are my best. But soon enough they all came, all the other birds, the moor-hens and coots, the crested grebes and the swans, the cormorants and the ducks. This morning I saw an egret too, perched on a buoy out in the river, and you don't see many of those. They're quite like herons, only much smaller, and white, snow-white. He was so beautiful. I couldn't take my eyes off him.

I was watching him through my binoculars, and he was looking right back at me. It was like he was asking me, "Hey you, what are you doing here? This is my river, don't you know?" Suddenly, without any warning, he lifted off. Then they all lifted off, all the birds on the shore, all the birds in the river. It was really strange. It was just as if I'd fired a gun or something, but I hadn't. I looked around. There wasn't a single bird anywhere. They'd all disappeared. For a while the river was completely still and empty and silent, like it was holding its breath almost, waiting for something that was about to happen. I was doing the same.

Then I spotted something slicing slowly through the water towards me. It was a fin. Shark! I thought. Shark! And a warm shiver of fear crept up my back. Then I saw the head and knew at once it couldn't be a shark. It was more like a dolphin, but it wasn't. It wasn't quite the right shape. It was too big and too long to be a dolphin. It was big enough to be a whale, a real whale. Now I knew what it was. With a face like that I knew at once that it had to be a bottle-nosed whale. It's the only whale that's got a face like a dolphin. (I know quite a lot about whales because my uncle sent me a whale poster he'd got out of a newspaper, and I've had it pinned up in my bedroom over my bed ever since. So that's why I can recognise just about all the whales in the world, narwhals, belugas, sperm whales, pilot whales, minkies, bottle-nose whales, the lot.)

To begin with I just stood there and stared. I

thought I was still dreaming. I couldn't take it in. I couldn't believe my eyes. I mean, a whale in the Thames, a whale in Battersea! He was close to the shore now, in shallower water, and still coming towards me. I could see almost all of him, from his head to his tail. But after a bit, I could see he wasn't really swimming any more, he was just lying there in the shallows, puffing and blowing a bit from time to time. He must be resting, I thought, tired out after a long journey perhaps. And then I noticed he was watching me as hard as I was watching him, almost like he was trying to stare me out, except I could tell from the gentleness in his eye that he wasn't being unfriendly towards me. He was interested in me, that's all, as interested as I was in him.

That's when I knew – don't ask me how, I just knew – that he wanted me to come closer to him.

13

I climbed the wall and ran along the shore. The tide was already going out fast. I could see at once that he was in great danger. If he stayed where he was he'd soon be stranded. I was walking slowly, so as not to alarm him. Then I crouched down as close as I could get to him, the water lapping all around me. His great domed head was only just out of my reach. We were practically face-to-face, eye-to-eye. He had eyes that seemed to be able to look right into me. He was seeing everything I was thinking.

I was sure he was expecting me to say something. So I did.

"What are you doing here?" I asked him. "You're a bottle-nose whale, aren't you? You shouldn't be here at all. You don't belong in the Thames. On my whale poster it says you live in the North Atlantic somewhere. So you should be up there, near

16

Iceland, near Scotland maybe, but not down here. I've seen bottle-nose whales on the telly too, on Planet Earth I think it was. There were lots of you all together. Or maybe it was pilot whales, I can't remember. But anyway, you always go around in schools, don't you, in huge family groups. I know you do. So how come you're all alone? Where's the rest of you? But maybe you're not all alone. Maybe some of your family came with you, and you got yourself a bit lost. Is that it?"

He kept staring back at me out of his big wide eye. I thought the best thing I could do was to just keep talking. I couldn't think what else to do. For a moment or two I didn't know what else to say, and anyway I suddenly felt a bit stupid talking to him. I mean, what if someone was watching me? Luckily, though, there was no one about. So instead, I looked up river, back towards Battersea Bridge, to see if any of his family might have come with him, but everywhere the river was empty and glassy and still. There was nothing there, nothing that broke the surface anyway. He was alone. He'd come alone.

And that was when it happened. The whale spoke! I'm telling you the truth, honest. The whale spoke to me. His voice was like an echoing whisper inside my head, like a talking thought. But it was him talking. It really was, I promise you. "No," he said. "My family's not with me. I'm all on my own. They came some of the way with me, and they're waiting for me back out at sea. And you're right. We usually stay close to our families – it's safer that way. But I had to do this bit alone. Grandfather said it would be best. Grandfather would have come himself, but he couldn't. So I've come instead of him. Everyone said it was far too dangerous, that there was no point, that it's too late anyway, that people won't listen, that they just won't learn, no matter what. But Grandfather knew differently. He always said I should go, that time was running out, but there was still hope. I was young enough and strong enough to make the journey, he said. One of us had to come and tell you. So I came. There are some things that are so important that you just have to do them, whatever anyone says, however dangerous it might be. I believe that. And besides, I promised Grandfather before he died. I promised him I'd come and find you. And I always keep my promises. Do you keep your promises?"

I could just about manage a nod but that was all. I tried, but I couldn't speak a word. I thought maybe I was going mad, seeing things that weren't there, hearing voices that weren't real, and suddenly that really terrified me. That was why I backed away from him. I was just about ready to run off when he spoke again.

19

"It's all right," he said. "Don't be frightened. I want you to stay. I want you to listen to me. I've come a very long way to talk to you, and I haven't got long."

His tail thrashed suddenly, showering me with water, and that made me laugh. But then I could see it was serious. He was rolling from one side to the other, rocking himself violently. Now I saw what it was that he was struggling to do. He was trying to back himself out into deeper water, struggling to keep himself afloat. I wanted to help him, but I didn't know how. All I could do was stand there and watch from the shore. It took him a while before he was out into deeper water and able to swim free again. He was blowing hard. I could tell he'd given himself a terrible fright. He swam off into the middle of the river, and then just disappeared completely under the water.

I stood there for ages and ages, looking for him up

and down the river – he could have gone anywhere. I was longing for him to surface, longing to see him again, worried that he'd never dare risk it again. But he did, though when he came back towards me this time he kept his distance. Only his head was showing now, and just occasionally his fin. "I've got to watch it," he said. "The tide is going out all the time. Grandfather warned me about it, they all warned me. 'Stay clear of the shore', they told me. 'Once you're beached you're as good as dead.' We can breathe all right out of the water, that's not the problem. But we need water to float in. We can't survive long if we get stranded. We're big, you see, too heavy for our own good. We need water around us to survive. If we're not afloat we soon crush ourselves to death. And I don't want that to happen, do I?"

Maybe I got used to him speaking to me like this, I don't know. Or maybe I just wanted to hear more.

Either way, I just didn't feel at all scared any more. I found myself walking back along the shore to be closer to him, and crouching down again to talk to him. I had things I needed to ask him.

"But I still don't really understand," I said. "You said you'd come to talk to me, didn't you? That means you didn't get lost at all, did you?"

"No, I didn't get lost," he told me. "Whales don't get lost, well not that often anyway. We tell each other where we are all the time, what's going on all around the world. What we see we share. So each and everyone of us has a kind of map of the oceans, all the mountains and valleys under the sea, all the rivers and creeks, the coast of every continent, and every island, every rock – it's inside our heads. We grow up learning it. That's why we don't get lost." He paused for a while, puffing hard through his blowhole. Talking was exhausting for him, I could see that.

"But we do get tired," he went on, "and we get old too, and we get sick, just like people do. We've a lot more in common with people than you know. We've got this earth in common for a start – and that's why I've come all this way to see you. We don't just share it with whales, but with every living thing. With people too. I've come to help you to save yourselves before it's too late, because if you save yourselves, then you'll be saving us too. It's like Grandfather said: we can't survive without you and you can't survive without us."

I didn't have a clue what he was on about, but I didn't dare say so. But I felt his eye searching out my thoughts. "You don't really know what I'm talking about, do you?" I shook my head. "Then I think the best thing I can do is to tell you about Grandfather, because it all began with Grandfather. When I was little, Grandfather was always going off on his travels, voyages of discovery, he called them. All over the world he went. We hardly ever saw him. Sometimes he was away for so long we all thought he was never coming back, and he wasn't all that good about keeping in touch either. He was a sort of adventurer, my grandfather, an explorer. He liked to go to places where no whale had ever been before.

"Then one day - it was some time ago now, when I was quite little - he came back from his travels and told us an amazing story. Ever since I first heard that story, I dreamed of going where Grandfather had gone, of seeing what he had seen. Grandfather had gone off to explore an unknown river, to follow it inland as far as he could go. No other whale had ever before dared to go there, as far as anyone knew anyway. All he knew of this river was that a couple of narwhals had been beached there in the mouth of the river a long time ago.

They never made it back out to sea. The warning had gone out all over the oceans, and that was why whales had avoided the river ever since.

"It took a while for Grandfather to find it, but when he did he just kept on swimming. On and on he swam right into the middle of the biggest city he'd ever seen. It was teeming with life. Everywhere he looked there were great cranes leaning out over the river, and towering wharfs and busy docks. Everywhere there were boats and barges. He saw cars and trains and great red buses. And at night the lights were so bright that the whole sky was bright with them. It was a magical city, a place of bridges and towers and spires. And everywhere there were people, crowds of them, more than he'd ever seen before, more than he'd ever imagined there could be. He wanted to stay longer, to explore further upstream, to discover more. It was a wonderful place,

but Grandfather knew it was dangerous too. The further upriver he swam, the shallower the waters around him were becoming. There were boats and barges everywhere, and he knew that if he wasn't very careful any one of them could run him down, and be the death of him. When a propeller took a nick out of his fin, he decided it was time to leave. And besides, he was weak with hunger by this time. He knew he couldn't go any further.

"So he turned around and tried to swim back the way he'd come, back out to sea. But that was when he found that the tide was going down fast. He was having to keep to the deep channels, but so were all the boats and the barges of course. There was danger all around him. He was so busy looking out for boats, that he didn't notice how shallow the water was getting all around him. Grandfather knew, as all whales do, just how easy it is to get

30

yourself stranded. He always said it was his own fault that he got stranded. He lost concentration. But Grandfather got lucky. Some children saw him floundering there in the shallows, and came running down to the river to help him. They helped him back into the water, and then stayed with him till they were sure he was going to be all right. They saved his life, those children, and he never forgot it. 'When you get there, find a child,' he told me, 'because children are kind. They'll help you, they'll listen, they'll believe you.' So you see, it was only because of those children that Grandfather managed to find his way back out to the open sea again, and come back to us and tell us his story."

That was when I noticed that all the birds were back again, the egret too on his buoy out in the river. They had gathered nearby. There were pigeons and blackbirds perching on the trees behind me. On the shore not far away from me a beady-eyed heron stood stock still, and there was a family of ducks bobbing about on the river, a couple of cormorants amongst them, all looking at the whale but none of them too close. And like me, they were listening. Even the trees seemed to be listening.

The whale spoke again. "Grandfather told me exactly how to get here, just how many days south I had to swim. He said I had to look out for the fishing boats and their nets, not to hug the coastline, because that was where there were always more boats about. He warned me about the currents and the tides, told me where the deep channels were in the river, and not to show myself till I had to. I mustn't stay too long. I mustn't swim too far up river.

I mustn't go any further than I had to. 'You'll want to,' he told me, 'just like I did. When you find a child that'll be far enough. And when you find him, tell him all I've told you, what we whales all know and people refuse to understand. Tell him it's our last chance and their last chance. And you must make sure it's a child you tell. The old ones are greedy. They have hard hearts and closed minds, or they would not have done what they have done. They're too old to listen, too old to change. The young ones will listen and understand. Just like they saved me, they can save the world. If they know, they will want to put it right – I know they will. They just need telling. All you have to do is tell them.' That's what Grandfather told me. So that's why I have found you, and that's why I have come."

That was when I saw he was drifting closer and closer to the shore again. I was just about to warn him when he must have realised the danger himself, because suddenly his tail began to thrash wildly in the shallows. The birds took off in a great flurry of panic. The whale didn't stop flailing around till he'd found his way back out into deeper waters, where he dived down and vanished altogether. This time I wasn't really that worried. I knew in my heart that he would come back, that he had much more to tell me. All the same, he was gone a long while before he appeared again, and I was so pleased to see him when at last he did.

It was the strangest thing, but when he began speaking to me again this time, I found I wasn't just hearing his words and understanding them. It was as if I could see in my mind everything he was telling me. I was seeing it all happen right there in front of my eyes. He wasn't just telling me. He was taking me round the world, round his world and showing me.

He showed me the bottom of the sea, where a coral reef lay dying and littered with rubbish. I saw a sperm whale being winched bleeding out of the sea, a leatherback turtle caught up in vast fishing nets, along with sharks and dolphins. There was an albatross too, hanging there limp and lifeless.

I saw the ice-cliffs in the Arctic falling away into the sea, and a polar bear roaming the ice, thin and hungry.

He showed me skies so full of smoke that day had become night, and below them the forests burning. An orang-utan was running for her life along a beach, clutching her infant, the hunters coming after her. I watched as they shot her down, and wrenched the screaming baby out of her arms. And then he showed me people, thousands upon thousands of them in a tented city by the sea, and a skeletal child lying alone and abandoned on the sand. She wasn't crying, because she was dead.

"Grandfather said all this killing has to stop. You are killing the sea we live in! You are killing the air we breathe. You are killing the world. Tell a child, Grandfather said. Only the children will put it right. That's why I came. That's why I found you. Will you put it right?"

"But how can I?" I cried.

"Tell them why I came. Tell them what I said. Tell them they have to change the way they live. And don't just tell them. Show them. Will you do that?"

"Yes," I cried. "I promise!"

"But do you keep your promises?" he asked.

"I'll keep this one," I told him.

"That's all I needed to hear," he said. "Time for me to go now. I don't want to get myself beached, do I? I like your town. I like your river. But I'm more at home back in my sea."

42

"But what if you are beached?" I asked. "What if you die?"

"I'd rather not, of course," he said. "But like I told you. I had to come. It was important, the most important thing I ever did. I promised I'd do it, didn't I? Now I've done it. The rest is up to you."

And away he swam then, blowing loudly as he passed upriver under Battersea Bridge, so that the whole river echoed with the sound of it. There was a final flourish of his tail before he dived. It was like he was waving goodbye, so I waved back. I stayed there watching for a while just in case he came up again. All around me the birds were watching too. But that was the last we saw of him.

And that's the end of my story.

Mrs Fergusson was so delighted to see Michael writing away that she let him go on long after the others had finished. That's why she let him stay in all through break-time too. She stayed in the classroom with him because she had some marking to do anyway. Every time she looked up Michael was still beavering away at his story. She'd never seen him so intent on anything, and certainly not on his writing. Until now, he'd always seemed to find writing rather difficult. She was intrigued. She was longing to ask him what he was writing about, but she didn't want to interrupt him.

Michael finished just as the bell went and everyone came rushing back into the classroom again, filling the place with noise. When they'd settled down Mrs Fergusson thought she'd try something she hadn't tried before with this class. She asked if any of them would like to read their story out loud to the rest of the class. It was the last thing Michael wanted. They wouldn't believe him. They'd laugh at him, he knew they would. So he was very relieved when Elena, who always sat next to him, put up her hand. He was quite happy to sit there and listen to another of Elena's horsey stories. Elena was mad about horses. It was all she ever wrote about or talked about, all she ever painted too. Mrs Fergusson said it was good, but a bit short, and that perhaps it might be nice if she wrote about something else besides horses once in a while. Michael was looking out of the window, thinking of his whale deep down in the sea with his family all around him. So it caught him completely by surprise when she suddenly turned to him, and said, "Well Michael, why don't you read us yours? What's it about?"

"A whale, Miss," Michael replied.

She was coming over to his table. She was picking up his book. "A whale? That sounds really interesting," she said. "Goodness gracious. You've written pages and pages, Michael. You've never written this much before, have you? Would you like to read it for us?" Michael shook his head, which didn't surprise Mrs Fergusson at all. Michael was never one to volunteer himself for anything. "Your handwriting is a bit squiggly, but I think I can read it." She leafed through the pages. "Yes, I'm sure I can. Shall I read it out for you? You don't mind, do you, Michael?" Then she spoke to the whole class. "Would you like to hear Michael's whale story, children?" And they all did, so there was nothing Michael could do to stop her.

He had to sit there and listen like everyone else. He wanted to put his hands over his ears. He didn't dare to look up. He didn't want to have to see all those mocking smiles. To begin with, Mrs Fergusson read it like she always did, in her teach-ery voice, as if it was just a story. Then gradually, her whole tone seemed to change, and she was reading it as if she was inside the story and down by the river, as if she was seeing it all, hearing it all, feeling it all, as if she was longing to know what was going to happen. Michael dared to look around him now. No one was laughing. No one was even smiling. The longer the story went on, the more Mrs Fergusson's voice trembled, and the more silent the class became. When she'd finished she stood there for a long while, so moved she was unable to speak. But Michael was still waiting for the first sound of laughter, dreading it. Then, all of a sudden, Elena started clapping beside him, and moments later they were all clapping, including Mrs Fergusson who was smiling at him through her tears.

"An amazing story, Michael, the best I've read in a long, long time – and certainly the best you've ever written. Quite wonderful," she said. "Only one thing I would say, Michael," she went on. "It doesn't really matter of course, but if you remember, Michael, I did tell you it had to be a true story, about something that really happened."

"It is true, Miss," Michael told her. "It all happened, just like I said. Honest."

That's when Jamie Bolshaw started sniggering and snorting. It spread all around the classroom until everyone was laughing out loud at him. It didn't stop until Mrs Fergusson shouted at everyone to be quiet.

"You do understand what 'true' means, Michael, don't you?" she said. "It means not made up. If it is true, as you say it is, then that means that right now, just down the road, there's a bottle-nose whale swimming about in the river. And it means you actually met him, that he actually talked to you."

"Yes, Miss. He did, Miss," Michael said. "And I did meet him, this morning, early. Promise. About half past five, or six. And he did talk to me. I heard his voice and it was real. I wasn't making it up. But he's not there any more, Miss, because he's gone back out to sea, like I said. It's true, all of it. I promise you, Miss. It was just like I wrote it." And when Jamie Bolshaw started tittering again, Michael felt tears coming into his eyes. Try as he did, he couldn't hold them back, nor could he hold back the flood of words. He so wanted to make them believe him.

"It's true, Miss, really true. When it was all over I ran all the way back home. Mum was already having her breakfast. She told me I was late, that

I'd better hurry or I'd be late for school. I told her why I was late. I told her all about the whale, the whole thing. She just said it was a good story, but that she didn't have time for stories just now, and would I please sit down and eat my breakfast. I said it was all true, every word of it. I crossed my heart and hoped to die. But she didn't believe me. So I gave up in the end and just ate my breakfast like she said.

"And when I got to school I didn't dare tell anyone, because I thought that if Mum didn't believe me, then no one else would. They'd just laugh at me, or call me a liar. I thought it would be best to keep quiet about it. And that's what I would have done. But you said we all had to write about something that had really happened to us. It could be funny or sad, exciting or frightening, whatever we wanted, you said, but it had to be true, really true.

'No fantasy, no science fiction, and none of your shock-horror stories, Jamie Bolshaw, none of that dripping blood stuff. I want you to write it down just as it happened, children, just as you remember it.' That's what you told us.

"And I couldn't think of anything else to write about except my whale. So that's what I wrote about. It was very long, the longest story and the most important story I've ever written. That's because I didn't want to leave anything out. I don't usually like writing stories. I'm no good at them. Can't get started, can't find a good ending. But this time it was like it was writing itself almost. All I had to do was to let it flow onto the page, down from my head, along my arm, through my fingers. Sometimes though, it was really hard to concentrate, because I kept thinking about my whale, hoping and hoping he was out in the open sea by now, with his family again, safe again. The more I hoped it, the more I believed it, and the more I believed it the more I wanted to tell his story. That's why I stayed in all through break-time to get it finished. It was raining anyway, so I didn't really mind."

When he'd finished there was a long silence.

"Yeah, yeah," Jamie sneered.

"That'll be quite enough of that, Jamie," Mrs Fergusson snapped, clapping her hands for silence. She could see now how upset Michael was becoming. "All right Michael, all right. We'll say no more about it for the moment. Now children, what I want is for you to illustrate the story you've just written. Like that poem poster on the wall above the bookshelf - the tiger one, over there. I read it to you last week, remember? 'Tiger, tiger, burning bright'. I told you, didn't I?

The poet illustrated it himself. And that's what I want you to do."

Through blinding tears Michael drew his bottle-nose whale, with the birds all around, the heron and the ducks and the cormorants, and the snowy white egret watching from the buoy. Then he drew himself, crouching down by the river's edge, with the sun coming up over London, all just as he'd seen it that morning. He had almost finished when, very surreptitiously, and making sure Mrs Fergusson wasn't looking, Elena slipped him a folded piece of paper. Michael opened it and read it. "Liar, liar, pants on fire." Elena was shaking her head and pointing at Jamie Bolshaw, who was making a face at him. That was the moment Michael lost it. He scrunched up the paper, got up, walked across the classroom and hurled it at Jamie's grinning face. "I'm not a liar," he screamed at him. "I'm not, I'm not!"

Mrs Fergusson put Jamie in one corner and Michael in another. They hadn't been there five minutes before Mr Jenner, the Headteacher, came in. Much to Michael's surprise and relief he didn't seem even to notice him standing there in the corner. He was pulling on his hat and coat. He was clearly going somewhere, and in an almighty hurry too. "Mrs Fergusson," he was saying. "I want your class to stop whatever it is that they're doing right now. I want them to get their coats on and assemble at once in the playground. And hurry please."

"Why? What's going on?" Mrs Fergusson asked. "Is it a fire drill?"

"No no, nothing like that. You're not going to believe this," Mr Jenner said, "but apparently there's a huge great whale in the river, right here, right now, just down the road from us. It's true. Not every day a whale comes to town, is it? It's on the telly. But we can see it for real. So I thought we'd all go and take a look. Quick as you can please, else he could be gone before we get there, and we don't want that, do we?" And then he was gone.

Everyone was gaping at Michael. For some time after Mr Jenner had left, no one said a word, not even Mrs Fergusson. But in spite of the look of utter amazement on Jamie Bolshaw's face, Michael could not for one moment enjoy his triumph. All he could think of was that his whale hadn't made it to the sea, that he must still be floundering in the river, still there, and trapped. He knew only too well what that might mean. He had to be there, now. He was out of the classroom, across the playground already full of excited children being herded into lines, and on his way down to the river before anyone could stop him.

By the time Michael arrived, there were crowds

everywhere, hundreds of them lining the river on both sides, and all along Battersea bridge too. He pushed though the crowds and hoisted himself up onto the wall so he could see over. There were police down on the shoreline keeping everyone back behind the wall. From the first moment he saw the whale Michael could see he was in serious trouble. He was wallowing helpless in the shallows, at the mercy of the tide, unwilling or unable to move.

Standing next to Michael was a building worker in a yellow hard-hat and muddy boots. He was screaming down his mobile phone. "It's huge! Humungous, I'm telling you. Looks more like a bleeding shark to me. And he's going to get himself well and truly stuck in the mud if he's not careful, and that'll be his lot. Yeah, just below Battersea Bridge. I've got my yellow hat on, you can't miss me. I'll look out for you. No, he'll still be here. He's not going anywhere, poor blighter. And don't forget to bring the camcorder, right? This won't happen again. Once in a lifetime this."

There were half a dozen people around the whale, a couple of divers amongst them, trying to encourage him back into the water, but Michael could see it was no use. Without him the whale seemed to have lost all will to live. He was trying to decide what he could do, how he could get to the whale without being stopped by the police, when he found Mr Jenner beside him and Mrs Fregusson too, both breathless.

"You shouldn't have gone running off like that, Michael," said Mrs Fergusson. "You had us worried sick."

"He needs me," Michael told her. "I've got to go to him."

"You leave it to the experts," said Mr Jenner. "Come on over with the other children now. We've got a great view where we are."

"I don't want a great view," Michael shouted. "Don't you understand? I have to save him."

Michael didn't think twice after that. He climbed over the wall and raced along the shore towards the whale, dodging the police as he went. When Mr Jenner tried to call him back, Mrs Fergusson put her hand on his arm. "Best leave him be," she told him. "It's his whale. I'll go after him."

By the time the police managed to catch up with Michael, Mrs Fergusson was there to explain everything. They took some persuading, but in the end they said they could make an exception just this once, provided she stayed with him all the time, and provided both of them wore lifejackets, and didn't interfere.

So, along with several others, Michael and Mrs Fergusson were there when the tide began to rise, and at last the whale began to float free of the mud. Michael stayed as close to his head as he could get, and talked to him all the while to reassure him. "You'll be all right now," he said. "There's lots of us here, and we all want to help you. You'll swim out of here just like your grandfather did. All you have to do is swim. You must swim. You've got your whole family waiting for you out there. Do it for them. Do it for me."

They walked knee high with the whale out into the river, one of the divers swimming alongside him the whole time. Michael could see how hard the whale was trying. He was trying all he could, but he was so weak. Then, to the rapturous cheers of everyone around the whale seemed suddenly to find strength enough to move his tail, and he managed to swim away from the shore, blowing hard as he went. They watched him turning slowly out in the middle of the river. And when everyone saw he was swimming the right way, another huge cheer went up. But Michael just wished they'd keep quiet. He sensed that all this noise must be bewildering and disorientating for him. But when the whale swam away under the bridge back towards the sea, even Michael joined in the cheering.

Like everyone else, when the whale dived down

and disappeared, Michael thought he would be all right now, that he was well and truly on his way, that he'd make it this time for sure. But for some reason, by the time the whale surfaced again, he had turned and was coming back towards them. Within no time at all he had drifted back into the shallows, and despite all they tried to do to stop him, he had beached himself again.

Mrs Fergusson tried to stop him, so did the others, but Michael broke free of them and waded as far out into the river as he could, until he was as near to him as he could get. "You've got to swim!" he cried. "You've got to. Go under the bridge and just keep going. You can do it. Don't turn around. Don't come back. Please don't come back!"

There were people and boats everywhere, bustle and ballyhoo all around, so much of it that Michael could barely hear the whale when he spoke. "I'm trying," he said. "I'm trying so hard. But I'm very tired now, and I don't seem to know where I'm going any more. I'm feeling muddled in my head, and I'm so tired. I just want to sleep. I'm afraid that maybe I stayed too long. Grandfather warned me, they all warned me." His eyes closed. He seemed almost too exhausted to say anything more. Then his eyes opened again. "You do remember everything I said?" he whispered.

"Of course I do. I'll never forget. Never."

"Then it was worth it. No matter what happens, it was worth it. Stay with me if you can. I need you with me."

So Michael did stay. He stayed all that day, and Mrs Fergusson stayed with him, long after all the other children had gone back home. By late afternoon his mother was there with them - they'd got a message to her at work. And the white egret stayed too, watching everything from his buoy.

As evening came on they tried to make Michael go home to sleep for a while.

"There's nothing more you can do here," his mother told him. "And anyway, you can watch it on the television. You can't stay here all night. You'll catch your death. We'll get a pizza on the way. What do you say?" Michael stayed crouching down where he was. He wasn't moving.

"I tell you what, Michael," Mrs Fergusson said, "I'll stay. You go home and get some rest, and then you can come back in the morning. I won't leave him, honestly I won't. And I'll phone if anything happens. How's that?"

Between them they managed to persuade him. Michael knew everything they said was true. He was tired, and he was cold, and he was hungry. So in the end he agreed, just so long as he could come back in the morning, at first light, he said.

"I won't be long," he whispered to the whale. "I'll be back soon, I promise."

Back at home in a hot bath he shivered the cold out of him, but all the while he was thinking only of his whale.

He ate his pizza watching his whale on the television. He knew he couldn't go to bed. He didn't want to sleep. He wanted only one thing, to be back down by the riverside with his whale. He begged his mother again and again to let him go, but she wouldn't let him. He had to get some sleep, she said.

There was only one thing for it. He would wait till his mother had gone to bed, then he'd get dressed and slip out of the flat. That's what he did. He ran all the way back down to the river.

All the rescue team and the divers were still there, and so was Mrs Fergusson, sitting by the wall wrapped in a blanket. And everywhere there were still dozens of onlookers. The egret was there on his buoy. And the whale was floundering near the shore, not far from where Michael had left him. But there was something else out on the river. It looked like a barge of some kind, and it hadn't been there before - Michael was sure of it. He ran over to Mrs Fergusson.

"Miss, what's that barge there for?" he asked her. "What's going on?"

"They're going to lift him, Michael," she said. "They had a meeting, and they decided it's the only way they can save him. They don't think he can do it on his own, he's too weak and too disorientated. So they're going to lift him onto that barge and carry him out to sea."

"They can't!" Michael cried. "They'll kill him if

they do. He can't live out of the water, he told me so. He's my whale. I found him. They can't, they mustn't! I won't let them!"

Michael didn't hesitate. He dashed down to the shore and waded out into the river. When he found he couldn't wade any more, he began to swim. A few short strokes and he was alongside the whale. He could hear Mrs Fergusson and the others shouting at him to come back. He paid them no attention. The whale looked at him out of his deep dark eye.

"I need you with me," he whispered.

"I know. I'm back," Michael said. "Are you listening? Can you hear me?"

"I hear you," replied the whale.

"I'm going to swim with you," Michael told him. "I'm a really good swimmer. We're going together. You just have to follow me. Can you do that?"

"I'll try," said the whale.

From the bank they all saw it, Michael and the whale swimming away side by side towards Battersea Bridge. They could hardly believe their eyes. They could see the whale was finding it hard, puffing and blowing as he went, that Michael was battling against the tide. But incredibly, they were both making some headway. By now the rescue team had sent out an inflatable to fetch Michael in. Everyone could see what was bound to happen in the end, that the tide was against them, that it was too cold, that it was impossible. Both the boy and the whale tired together. They hauled Michael out of the water, and brought him back to the shore. From there he had to watch his whale swim on bravely for a few more minutes, before he had to give up the unequal struggle. Even Michael knew now that there was nothing more he could do, that the barge was the whale's only chance of survival.

* * *

Michael was there on the shore with his mother and Mrs Fergusson later that morning when they hoisted the whale slowly out of the water, and swung him out in a great sling onto the barge that would take him out to sea. With the world watching on television, followed by a procession of small boats, the barge carried him along the river, under the bridges, past Westminster and the London Eye and St Pauls, out towards Greenwich and the Thames Barrier and to the sea beyond. There was a vet on hand to monitor his progress all the way. And Michael too never left the whale's side, not for one moment. He stayed by him, pouring water over him from time to time, to keep his skin moist, soothing him and talking to him to reassure him, to keep his spirits up, all the while hoping against hope that the whale would have

79

the strength to survive long enough to reach the open sea.

Michael didn't have to ask, he could see the vet was not optimistic. He could see his whale was failing fast. His eyes were closed now, and he had settled into a deep sleep. He was breathing, but only barely. Michael thought he did hear him breathe just one more word.

"Promise?" he said.

"I promise" Michael replied. He knew exactly what he was promising, that he would spend his whole life keeping it. And then the whale simply stopped breathing. Michael felt suddenly very alone.

The vet was examining him. After a while he looked up, wiping the tears from his face. "Why?" he asked. "I don't understand. Why did he come? That's what I'd like to know."

Ahead of them, as they came back into the

heart of London, flew a single white bird. It was
the snowy white egret that had never left the
the whole way out and the whole way back.
The whole of London seemed still
with sadness as they passed by
under Tower Bridge.

AUTHOR'S NOTE

On 20 January 2006, an eighteen-foot
(five metre) northern bottle-nosed whale was
spotted swimming up the Thames past the
Houses of Parliament. She swam up as far as
Battersea Bridge where she became stranded.
For two days rescuers battled to save the whale,
as the world looked on, hoping for the best.
But in spite of everyone's efforts the whale
died before the rescue pontoon on which
she was being transported could reach
the safety of the open sea.

Michael Morpurgo

I BELIEVE IN UNICORNS

Walker Books will donate a percentage of the royalty from the sale of this book to the Unicorn Theatre, which opened in 2005 as the first purpose-built professional theatre for children in the UK.

First published 2005 by Walker Books Ltd, 87 Vauxhall Walk, London SE11 5HJ

This edition published 2006

10 9 8 7 6

Text © 2005 Michael Morpurgo
Illustrations © 2005 Gary Blythe

The right of Michael Morpurgo and Gary Blythe to be identified as author and
illustrator respectively of this work has been asserted by them in accordance with
the Copyright, Designs and Patents Act 1988

This book has been typeset in Centaur

Printed in China

British Library Cataloguing in Publication Data: a catalogue record for this book
is available from the British Library

ISBN 978-1-4063-0204-2

www.walker.co.uk

I BELIEVE IN UNICORNS

Michael Morpurgo

Illustrated by Gary Blythe

WALKER BOOKS
AND SUBSIDIARIES
LONDON · BOSTON · SYDNEY · AUCKLAND

To my grandsons, Alan and Laurence — M.M.

My name is Tomas Porec. I was just eight years old when I first saw the unicorn, and that was twenty long years ago.

I grew up and live to this day in a mountain village that we like to think is just about big enough to call itself a small town. Hidden away in a remote valley it might seem to travellers passing through that it is far too sleepy for anything of any significance ever to have happened here. Not so, for something very significant did happen, something both dreadful and wonderful at the same time.

For me as a child this place was my whole world, a place full of familiar wonders. Being an only child I spent a lot of time wandering about on my own. I knew every cobbled alleyway, every lamppost. I knew all the houses, and I knew everyone who lived in them too — and their dogs. And they knew me. From my bedroom window in the farmhouse where we lived on the edge of town, I could look out over the rooftops to the church tower. I loved to watch the swifts screaming around it in swooping squadrons on summer evenings. I loved the deep dong of the church bell that lingered long in the air. But as for going to church,

that was a different matter. If ever I could get out of it I most certainly would. I'd far rather go fishing with Father. He didn't like church any more than I did. Mother and Grandma always went, religiously.

But church or not, Sunday was always the best day of the week. In the cold of winter Father and I would go tobogganing on the hillside. In the heat of the summer we'd swim in the lakes and stand there under the freezing

waterfalls, laughing and squealing with joy. Sometimes we'd go off for long tramps up in the hills. We'd watch the eagles soaring out above the mountain tops. We'd wander the forests, always on the lookout for telltale signs of deer or wild boar, or even bears. Sometimes we might even catch a brief glimpse of one through the trees. Best of all we'd stop from time to time, just to be still, to feel the peace and breathe in the beauty. We'd listen to the sounds of the forest, to the whisper of the wind, to the cry of wolves, distant wolves I longed to see but never did.

There'd be picnics too, with all of us there. Grandma, Mother, Father and me, and while they slept afterwards, stretched out in the sun, I'd go rolling down the hills, over and over, and end up lying there breathless on my back, giddy with happiness, the clouds and mountains spinning all about me.

I didn't like school any more than I liked church. But

Mother was much more strict with me about school than she ever was about church. Father took my side in all this. He always said that school and books had never done him much good, and that Mother fussed me too much. "A day in the mountains will teach him a whole lot more than a week in school," he'd say. But Mother was adamant. She never let me miss a day of it, no matter how much I complained of stomach-ache or headache. I could never fool Mother – I don't know why I went on bothering even to try. She knew me and my little games far too well. She knew I'd lie shamelessly, invent anything not to have to go into that school playground and line up with the others, not to have to face the four walls of the classroom again, not to have to face the teachers' endless questions, nor the mocking banter of my friends when I made mistakes, which I very often did. So there I'd find myself, day after day, wishing away the hours, gazing out at the mountains and forests where I so longed to be.

As soon as school was over each afternoon, I ran straight back home for my bread and honey, and then I was out to play as quick as I could. Not that I didn't like my bread and honey. I adored it. I was always so hungry after school. And besides, Mother baked the best bread in the world, and Father made the best honey too, or rather his bees did. Father was a beekeeper, as well as a bit of a farmer too. We had a little farm, a few goats on the hillside, some pigs and hens in the farmyard and a couple of cows too, but honey was his main business. He kept dozens of beehives all over the mountain slopes, so there was always plenty of honey. I never tired of it, especially the honeycomb, even though the waxy bits stuck in my teeth afterwards. Much less welcome was the mug of milk that Mother always forced me to drink before she let me go out to play. "Fresh from the cow," she'd say. "Good for you." Good for me or not I hated milk with a passion.

But I learnt to swallow it down fast, so fast that I hardly tasted it, knowing that the quicker I got it over with the sooner I could be up in my beloved mountains again. Sometimes I'd go off with Father, feeding the bees in winter, collecting the honey in summer. I loved that, loved being with him, doing a proper job. But although I never told him so, I much preferred to be on my own. Alone I could go where I wanted. Alone my thoughts and dreams could run free. I could sing at the top of my voice. I could soar with the eagles, be wild in the woods with the deer and the boar and bears and the invisible wolves. Alone I could be myself.

Then one afternoon after school I was just finishing off my mug of milk when I noticed Mother putting on her coat to go out. "I need to do some shopping, Tomas. D'you want to come with me?"

"I hate shopping," I told her.

"I know you do, Tomas," she said. "That's why I thought I'd take you down to the library. It'll be something different for you. It's all miserable and wet out there today. You don't want to be running about outside in weather like this."

"I do," I told her. But I knew she wasn't listening.

"You'll get soaked through, Tomas. You'll catch your death. And anyway you're always out there clambering around up in those mountains. You want to watch out you know. You go on like that and you'll grow four legs and a pair of horns, and I'll end up with a goat for a son. No, just for once you can go to the library instead. Don't worry, you won't have to come shopping with me. I'll go off and do the shopping on my own, whilst you go to the library and listen to some stories. Apparently there's this new librarian lady and she tells lovely stories. It'll be fun."

"It won't be fun," I said. "I hate stories. And anyway

stories aren't lovely. We have them at school." Already I could tell that Mother had made up her mind about this. Already I knew this was another battle I was not going to win. Even so, I was determined to go down fighting. I was still protesting vehemently as she put on my coat. "It'll be good for you, Tomas. Everyone says this new librarian lady is really wonderful. She does it every afternoon, tells stories to any children who want to listen."

"But I don't want to listen," I protested. It didn't do me any good.

"Well you won't know that until you've heard her, will you, Tomas?" By now she had me firmly by the hand and we were out of the house and hurrying down the road in the rain. She wasn't pulling me along exactly – she wouldn't have done that – but I was dragging my feet all I could, making as much of a nuisance of myself as possible, just so she'd know I wasn't giving in that easily, just to show how deep was my indignation at her outrageous infringement of my liberty. In the end though, and partly because people were watching, I gave up the unequal

struggle and went along with her as quietly as a lamb all the way down the main street and past the Town Hall. Mother walked me up the steps and into the entrance hall of the library, took off my coat and shook it dry. "Off you go, Tomas," she said, smoothing my hair. "I'll be back for you in an hour or so, all right? Enjoy yourself. Be good." And she was gone.

Even now I still hesitated. Through the glass doors

I could see there was an excited huddle of children gathering in the far corner of the library. Most of them were from my school. Frano with the sticking up hair was

there, and Anna, Christina, Dani and Antonio and a dozen others. None of them were in my class. None of them were my friends at all. Every one of them was younger than me. Some were too small to come to school at all – 'little snotties' as Father always called children of that age. I absolutely did not want to be sitting and listening to stories with a bunch of 'little snotties'. I had just about decided I wasn't going to stay, that I'd leave before anyone saw I was there, that I'd run up into the hills and face Mother's fury later, when I noticed they were jostling one another as if suddenly desperate to get a better look at something. It had to be something very interesting, that was for sure, and since I could not see what it was they were all getting so frantic about, I thought I'd move a little closer. So I found myself being drawn inside the main library and walking past the bookshelves towards this excited huddle of children in the corner.

Wanting to keep well out of sight, I half hid myself behind a bookshelf and looked on from a safe distance. As I watched, the children began to settle down, each of them finding a place to sit on the carpet. Then, quite improbably and inexplicably, they were all hushed, and still and attentive. That was the moment I first saw him, sitting there in the corner beyond the children. A unicorn! A real live unicorn! He was sitting absolutely still, his feet tucked neatly underneath him, his head turned towards us. He seemed to be gazing straight at me. I swear his eyes were smiling at me too. He was pure white as unicorns are, white head, body, mane and tail, white all over except for his golden horn and his little black hooves. And his eyes were blue and shining. It was some moments before I realized he was in fact not real, not live at all. He was too still to be real, his gaze was too constant and stony.

I suddenly felt very cross with myself for having been so stupid as to believe he could have been alive in the first place. Unicorns weren't actually real, I knew that much. Of course I did. It was quite obvious to me now that this was in fact a wooden unicorn. He had been carved out of wood and painted. But even as I came closer he seemed so lifelike. He looked so much how a unicorn should be, so magical and mysterious, that if he'd got to his feet and trotted off I still wouldn't have been in the least surprised.

Beside the unicorn, and just as motionless, there now stood a lady with a bright, flowery scarf around her shoulders, her hand resting on the unicorn's flowing mane. She must have noticed me skulking there by the bookshelf, still hesitant, still undecided, because suddenly she was beckoning me to

join them. Everyone had turned to stare at me now. I decided I would make a run for it, and began to back away. "It's all right," she said. "You can come and join us if you'd like to."

So it was that I found myself moments later sitting cross-legged on the floor with the others, watching her and waiting. She was patting the unicorn and smoothing his neck. She sat down on him then, but very carefully. She was treating him as if he was real, as if she didn't want in any way to alarm him. She gentled him, brushing his forehead with the back of her hand. Her hand, like the rest of her, was small and delicate and elegant. All around me now was the

silence of expectation. No one moved. Nothing happened. No one said anything.

Suddenly the girl sitting next to me — Anna it was — spoke up. "The unicorn story, Miss! We want the unicorn story!" Now everyone was clamouring for the same story. "The unicorn story! The unicorn story!"

"Very well, children," said the lady, holding up her hand to quieten everyone down. "We'll begin with the unicorn story then." She paused, closed her eyes for a few moments. Then opening them and looking straight at me, she began. "Look out of the window, children. It's raining isn't it? Have you ever wondered what would happen if the rain never stopped? This is a story about what happened a long, long time ago when one day it started to rain, and never stopped. It just went on and on. It all began because God was very angry at the world, because he saw the world was full of wicked people who didn't care about one another, nor for the beautiful world in which they lived. They had become cruel and selfish and greedy, and God wanted to teach all of them a lesson they would never forget. He decided there was only one way to do this. He would destroy all those wicked people, but he needed to be sure that the few people that were good and kind would survive, and the animals too – after all, the animals had never done anyone any harm, had they? This way he would be giving the world a second chance, a completely new start.

"So God chose the wisest and kindest man he could find. He was an old man called Noah. He told Noah he must build himself a great ship, a wooden ark, and he must begin it right away, and he had to make it big, the biggest ark ever built, because there had to be room not just for Noah and his family, but for two of every kind of animal on earth. So Noah and his family cut down the tallest trees. They sawed the wood into planks and began to build a huge ark, a gigantic ark, exactly as God had told him."

The lady on the unicorn was speaking so softly that I had to lean forward to hear her. I didn't want to miss a single word. "Of course," she went on, "all their neighbours thought they were barking mad to be building a ship in the middle of the countryside, off their heads, doolally. But that didn't bother Noah and his family, not one bit. They just ignored them and went right on building. It took them years and years to build such a huge ark, but finally when it was done they set about finding the animals. Two by two they brought them in, one male, one female of every kind of animal you can think of. There were lions and tigers, elephants and giraffes, cows, pigs, sheep, horses, deer, foxes, badgers, wolves and bears, wombats and wallabies — and bees and butterflies and grasshoppers too, insects of every sort. But, no matter how hard they searched they could not find any unicorns anywhere, not even one.

"Now Noah's grandchildren (and he had plenty of them) especially loved unicorns, as all children do. They spent weeks and months scouring the countryside all around looking just for unicorns. By now the rain was beginning to fall, a hard, heavy rain, a driving rain, a lashing rain, a constant rain, rain such as Noah and his family had never seen before. From the safety of the ark, filled now with two of every living creature on earth, except unicorns that is, Noah and all his family looked out and saw the lakes and rivers filling, saw the land flooding about them and felt the ark begin to float beneath them. Every valley was now a rushing, roaring torrent. All the towns and villages were swept away and all the wicked people with them. Still it rained and still it rained, until all that was left of the land were a few distant mountain tops.

"Inside the ark Noah and his family might have been safe, but they were not at all happy, his grandchildren in particular. 'What about the unicorns?' they cried, time and again. 'We haven't saved the unicorns.'

"They were quite inconsolable, until Noah came up with a wonderful idea. 'Why don't I make you one?' he said.

'I'll carve it out of wood. It'll look almost the same as a real one. You'll be able to sit on it, you'll be able to ride it. And unicorns are supposed to be lucky creatures, magical creatures, aren't they? It'll bring us luck and we're going to need luck on this journey, lots of it.' So to keep the children happy Noah carved them a unicorn, and like this one, it was splendid and beautiful and magical. The children loved to play on the unicorn, and sometimes Noah himself would sit on it and tell them stories, stories they loved, stories they would never forget.

"It wasn't Noah's fault, nor his children's, nor his grandchildren's. They were all busy down below feeding the animals in the ark. They didn't see, they didn't know that high on a nearby mountain top watching the ark drift right past them, stood the last two unicorns left alive on this earth. How they neighed and whinnied. How they reared up and pawed the air with their hooves. They tossed their heads and shook their manes, but it was no use. All too soon the ark had disappeared over the horizon. So the unicorns were left there stranded on the mountain top in the wind and rain, with nothing all around them but the heaving sea. Lightning forked and flashed through the clouds. Thunder rolled and rumbled around the world. Twisting tornadoes whipped the sea into a frenzy of fury. The great flood was spreading out over all the Earth and drowning it.

"As for the poor, stranded unicorns, the waters rose and rose around them until first their hooves were covered, then their backs, so that in the end, like it or not, they simply had to swim. They swam and they swam for hours, for days, for weeks. Then at last, at long last, the rain stopped, and the skies cleared above them. But still there was no land in sight. The unicorns swam on and on, hoping always to find land. But they never did.

"Far away and quite unbeknown to the unicorns, Noah's ark had come to rest on the top of Mount Ararat. Noah let the animals go as God had told him he should, two by two, so that once again the Earth would be filled

with creatures of all kinds, from grasshoppers to giraffes. From the wood of the ark, Noah built himself a house, while his family spread out all over the world. And now all these years later, children, there are millions and millions of us, including me, and you. So in a way we're all Noah's children, if you see what I'm saying."

No one spoke for a moment or two. Then someone said: "What happened to the two unicorns, Miss?"

"I was coming to that," she replied. "Those unicorns, they swam and they swam so far, for so long, for so many

years that in the end they didn't need their legs any more at all. And slowly, slowly, very slowly they turned themselves into whales. This way they could swim more easily. This way they could dive down to the bottom of the sea to feed whenever they wanted, and of course whenever they wished they could come up for air again. But in all this time they never

lost their magical powers, and they never lost their horns either. Which is why there really are to this very day whales in the sea with unicorn's horns. We call them narwhals." She leaned forward, her voice dropping to a whisper. "And sometimes, children, when they've had enough of the great, wide ocean and long to see children again and hear their laughter – unicorns particularly love children because they know that children particularly love them – they swim up onto the beaches on bright moonlit nights, and become unicorns once more, wonderful, magical unicorns, like this one. So I believe in them absolutely."

For some time after she had finished no one spoke a word. It was as if we were all waking up from a dream none of us wanted to leave. There were more stories after this, and some poems too. She had a bag of books beside her on the floor, her 'special books' she called them, the ones she loved best. Sometimes she would read from these books. Sometimes she would make up stories herself, or perhaps she knew them by heart – I wasn't sure which. It was the same with any story she told, every poem she recited, I just never wanted it to end. And when she finished each one, all I wanted was more.

"Now children," she said, closing the book she had been reading from. "Now it's your turn. Who would like to tell us a story today?"

A hand went up at once. It was Frano with the sticking up hair. "Me, Miss," he said, "Can I tell a story, Miss?" And so Frano told us a story about a duck that couldn't quack like other ducks, and could only talk instead, and how the other ducks laughed at him for being stupid, because he couldn't quack like they did. After Frano's story, there was Anna's, and then another and another. Everyone, it seemed, wanted their turn on the magical unicorn. I longed to have a try, but at the same time I was scared stiff. It wasn't just that I was frightened of making a fool of myself, I was simply terrified of being out there and talking in front of everyone. So I kept my hand down and let the others do it. The hour of stories flew by. On the way back home Mother asked me if I had enjoyed myself, if the stories had been good. "All right, I suppose," I conceded gracelessly. Well I wasn't going to give her the satisfaction, was I?

But at school the next day I told some of my friends all about the Unicorn Lady – all the little snotties seemed to call her that – and about her amazing stories and the magical storytelling powers of the unicorn. I told them they should come along and hear her for themselves. They weren't impressed. I mean stories and poems weren't exactly cool amongst my friends at school; but out of curiosity, I think, one or two of them did come along with me to the library that afternoon. As it turned out one or two was enough, because one or two soon became a few and then a few became many. Day after day as word spread in the school playground about the Unicorn Lady, the little group in the library grew and grew, until there was a whole crowd of us there every afternoon. We would rush out of school and race each other down the street to the library to find a spare place on the carpet as close as possible to the unicorn and the Unicorn Lady. She never once disappointed us. Every story she told, even if it was one we'd heard before, held us enthralled. It was the way she told them, I think, as if each of us was the only one she was talking to, and as if each story must be real and true, however unlikely, however fantastical. You could tell she believed absolutely in her stories as she told them. So we did too. Each day I wanted so much to take my turn on the magical unicorn and tell everyone a story, like the others were doing. But I could never banish my fear, never summon up the courage to put up my hand.

One afternoon – and that particular afternoon I had got to the library first and was sitting in the very best place on the carpet, right beside the unicorn – the Unicorn Lady reached into her bag of 'special' books and took out a book I'd never seen before. She held it up so we could all see. It looked rather old and tatty. The spine of the book was heavily taped, and the cover so stained that I found it difficult to read the title. And it was blackened too, at the edges, I noticed, as if it might have been scorched a long time ago.

"This, children," the Unicorn Lady said, "is definitely my most special book in all the world. It's my very own copy of *The Little Match Girl* by Hans Christian Andersen. You remember him, don't you? He was the author who wrote *The Ugly Duckling*, wasn't he? And *The Snow Queen*. This book may not look much to you, but my father gave it to me when I was a young girl. So it's very special to me. Very special indeed."

"Has it been burned, Miss?" I asked.

"Yes, Tomas."

"Why Miss, what happened?"

It was a while before she answered me. I saw a shadow of sorrow come across her face, and when she spoke at last her voice trembled so much I thought she might cry. "When I was little, even littler than any of you," she began, "I lived in another country far away from here. It was a time when wicked people ruled the land, wicked people who were frightened of the magic of stories and poems, terrified of the power of books. They knew, you see, that stories and poems help you to think and to dream. Books make you want to ask questions. And they didn't want any of us to think or dream, and especially they did not want us to ask questions. They wanted us only to think as they thought, to believe what they believed, to do as we were told. So one day in my town these wicked people went into all the bookshops and libraries and schools and brought out all the books they didn't like, which was most of them. And there in the square, soldiers in black boots and brown shirts built a huge bonfire of these books. As the books went up in flames, do you know what the soldiers did? They cheered.

Can you believe that, children? They cheered. I was there with my father watching it all happen."

"Suddenly I heard my father cry out; 'No! No!' And he rushed forward and plucked a book out of the fire. He tried to beat out the flames with his bare hands. The soldiers were shouting at us, so we ran away, but they came after us and caught up with us. They knocked my father to the ground and kicked him and hit him with sticks and rifle butts. My father curled up to protect himself as best he could, but he held on to the book and would not let go, no matter how much they beat him. They tried to tear it out of his hands, but he would not let them have it. This was the book he clung on to, children, this very book. This was the book he saved. So that is why it is my favourite, most special book in all the world." As she looked down at us, the shadow seemed slowly to lift from her, and she smiled. "And," she went on, *The Little Match Girl* also

happens to be a lovely story, children, very sad but very lovely. Tomas, I wonder if you'd like to come and sit on the unicorn and read it to us. You haven't had a turn on the unicorn yet, have you?" Everyone was looking at me. They were waiting. My mouth was dry. I couldn't do it. I was filled with sudden fear. "Come on," she said. "Come and sit beside me on the unicorn."

I had never been any good at reading out loud at school. I would forever stutter over my consonants – I dreaded k's in particular. Long words terrified me in case I pronounced them wrongly and everyone laughed at me. But now, sitting up there on the magic unicorn, I began to read, and all my dread and all my terror simply vanished. I heard my voice speaking out strong and loud. It was as if I was up in the mountains alone and singing a song at the top of my voice, for the sheer joy of the sound of it. The words danced like music on the air, and I could feel everyone listening. And I knew they were listening not to me at all, but to the story of *The Little Match Girl*, because they were just as lost in it as I was.

That same day I borrowed my first book from the library. I chose *Aesop's Fables* because I liked the animals in them, and because the Unicorn Lady had read them to us and I had loved them. I read them aloud to Mother that night when she came up to say goodnight to me. I read to her instead of her reading to me. It was the first time I'd ever done that. Father came and listened at the doorway whilst I was reading. He clapped when I'd finished. "Magic, Tomas," he said "That was magic." There were tears in his eyes too. I hoped it was because he was proud of me. How I loved him being proud of me. And Mother hugged me harder that night than she'd ever hugged me before. She could hardly speak she was so amazed. How I loved amazing Mother.

Then early one summer morning, war came to our valley. Before that morning I had known something of the war. But I didn't know what it meant, nor even why it was happening. I knew that some of the men from the town had gone to fight, Ivan Zec, the postman, Pavo Batina from the farm next to us, Tonio Raguz, Frano's brother, but I wasn't sure what for, nor where they had gone. For some time on the television I had been seeing soldiers riding through the streets on tanks, waving and smiling as they roared past, giving the thumbs up. I had asked Mother about it, and she told me that it was all far, far away down south, and I wasn't to worry myself, and besides, it would be over very soon. And on one of our long walks in the forest Father had told me that we would win in the end anyway and he promised me that war would never come to our town.

I remember the very moment it did come.

I was having my breakfast with sleep still in my head.

It was going to be a school day, an ordinary school day. As usual Mother was hassling me to hurry up and finish. Then as usual she sent me outside to open up the hens and feed them. We had a broody hen and I was just reaching in under her to see if her chicks had hatched out, when I heard the sound of a plane flying very low. I came out of the henhouse and saw it skimming over the rooftops. As I watched, it climbed, banked and came in again, glinting in the sunlight. It was very beautiful, like a huge, shining eagle, I thought. That was when the bombs began to fall, far away at first beyond the river, then closer, closer. Everything happened at once. Mother came running out of the house. Father had me by the hand. They were shouting at one another about who should fetch Grandma. Mother was screaming at us both to go, that she would go into town to find Grandma. Then Father and I were running out across the fields and up into the woods. Here we stayed hidden under the trees

and watched as the plane circled above us, as people came streaming out of town in their hundreds to join us in the woods. All the while we were hoping and hoping to see Mother and Grandma amongst them. But they didn't come and they didn't come. The plane dropped no more bombs now, but buzzed the town several times before soaring up over the mountains and away. When at long last we saw Mother and Grandma hurrying towards us over the fields, we were so relieved, so happy. We ran out from under the trees to help them. Back in the shelter of the forest we huddled together, all of us, arms around one another, our foreheads

pressed together, Grandma was praying out loud. Mother was rocking back and forth, not crying, but moaning, as if she was in pain. I was too frightened to cry, I think. That was when Father told us we had to promise to stay where we were until he came back to fetch us. He wasn't alone. There were a few other men with him. I watched them springing down the hillside towards the town. "Where's he going?" I asked. But Mother didn't answer me. She and Grandma were both on their knees now, their lips moving in silent prayer.

We did as Father had told us and stayed where we were. So we saw it all. Hidden high up in the forest, we could see the tanks and soldiers moving through the streets blasting and shooting as they came. There were fires burning now all over the town, so many that soon we could hardly see the houses for the smoke. Then came the silence. Had they gone? Was it over? I prayed then too. Please God let it be over. Please God don't let the soldiers come back. Please God keep Father safe. For long hours we all stayed where we were with the town burning below us, unsure what to do next.

When at last we did see one of the men running towards us up the hillside, it was not my father, but Frano's father. When he'd got his breath back he told us that the soldiers and tanks had all gone, that it was safe to go back home. "Where's Father?" I asked him.

"I don't know, Tomas," he said. "I haven't seen him."

Mother had to help Grandma down the hill, so I ran on ahead of them. I looked for Father at home, I called for him everywhere, but I couldn't find him. In the farmyard I found both our cows lying dead, the pigs too. There was blood, so much blood. The house itself had not been damaged, but there was terrible destruction all around me as I ran on into town searching for Father. I asked everyone I met if they had seen him, but no one had. Everyone was crying, and I was crying now because I couldn't forget the terrible sight of the cows and the pigs and the blood. Most of all I was beginning to fear the worst, that Father was dead and I'd never see him again.

The centre of the town had suffered the worst damage. There was hardly a building that hadn't been hit. The Town Hall was in flames, and every car in the streets was a blackened shell, some with the tyres still burning. There were men and women rushing everywhere trying to put out the fires, with hoses, with buckets, but Father wasn't amongst them. Others simply stood dazed in the streets looking about them. Some of them could hardly speak

when I asked them about Father. Old Mr Liban just shook
his head and wept.

And then I saw the library. There were flames licking
out of the upper windows. The fire engine was in the street,
the firefighters running out the hoses. "Have you seen my
father?" I asked them. "Have you seen my father?"

But before they could answer, I saw him for myself,
Father and the Unicorn Lady at the same moment. They
were coming out of the library, their arms piled high with
books. "I couldn't find you," I cried, running to him. "I
thought you were dead." I helped them set the books down

on the steps. Father put his arms around me then, and I held
him as tightly as he was holding me.

The Unicorn Lady was gazing up at the burning
building. "We must go back for more," she breathed, "I
won't let them burn the books. I won't."

When Father went with her back up the steps, I tried
to go too. "No, Tomas," Father told me, "You stay here
and look after the books we bring out." Then both of them
were running up the steps into the library, only to reappear
a couple of minutes later, their arms full of books again. A
crowd was beginning to gather in the square.

"We need help!" cried the Unicorn Lady. "We have to save the books."

That was the moment the great book rescue began. Suddenly there were dozens of people surging past me into the library. The firefighters warned that it was dangerous, but no one paid them any attention. It wasn't long before a whole book evacuation system had been set up. We children were organized into two human chains across the square, from the library itself to the café opposite, and all the rescued books went from hand to hand along the chains ending up piled in great stacks all over the floor of the café and on the tables too. When there was no more room in the café we used Mrs Danic's grocer's shop, and I remember Mrs Danic gave us free sweets, because we were all working so hard.

But the moment came when the firefighters at last had to put a stop to it all, and wouldn't let anyone else in to fetch out any more books. The ceilings could come down at any time, they said. "The unicorn," I cried, "What about the unicorn?" I needn't have worried. The last to emerge, faces smudged and smeared, eyes reddened, were the Unicorn Lady and Father, carrying the unicorn between them. He was blackened and burned on his back and his legs, and his tail was missing. But his face was still white and his horn still gold. They were staggering under his weight, so I dashed up the steps to help them. As we came down together everyone began applauding, and I knew the applause was for the unicorn as much as it was for us. The Unicorn Lady sat herself down on the unicorn choking so much she could hardly breathe. Mrs Danic brought her a glass of water. We children anxiously gathered all around her waiting for her to recover, waiting for her to speak. We were waiting for a story too, I think.

"I never told you this until now, children," she began, still coughing from time to time, her voice hoarse. "But

my father carved this unicorn for me when I was little. He always said it was every bit as magical as a real unicorn. So I always thought it was too, but now I know it for sure. The unicorn did it for us, children, protected the books in the library while the fire burned all around him. It was him that stayed with them, him that saved them." She smiled at us. "With a little help from his friends, of course."

She looked up at the library, at the fire now raging freely. "Don't worry children. We'll repair the unicorn, make him white again. As for the library, it's just a building. Buildings they can destroy. Dreams they cannot. Buildings you can always build again, and we shall build our library again just as it was, maybe better. Meanwhile we shall just have to find a way to look after all the wonderful books we have saved, won't we?"

"What about in my house?" said Frano. "We could keep some of them in my house."

"And mine." It was Anna this time.

"What a wonderful idea!" said the Unicorn Lady. "That's how we'll do it then. All of us who would like to, can take away all the books they can manage, and care for them. They must be kept dry, mind, and clean, and loved. Loved is very important. And when in one year to two or three this war is over and done with, when we have our new library again, then we can all bring back our books, and we'll carry the unicorn inside, and tell our stories once more. In the meantime we'll just have to find somewhere else to tell our stories, won't we?" She leaned forward so that we all listened even more carefully. "All we have to do, children, is to make sure this story comes true. You really have to believe something will happen before you can make it happen. And we will make it happen, because I told you this story sitting on the magical unicorn, didn't I?"

So it all turned out just as the Unicorn Lady said it

would. That evening every family, that still had a roof over their heads, took home a wheelbarrow full of books and looked after them. And there were people to look after too of course, people who had lost their houses, lost everything. Everyone was found a home somewhere. We had Frano and his family with us on our farm until they could rebuild their own place. It was a bit of a squash. I had to share my room with Frano and our pile of books. The books were fine, but Frano snored, which wasn't so fine.

The dark days of war did come to an end, and in time every house was rebuilt, and so was the library. It looked just the same as the old one, only newer of course. The unicorn was restored and repainted, and we all brought our books back and filled the library again. So the Unicorn Lady's story came true, just as she'd said it would.

The day the new library was officially opened — and because, I suppose, Father and I had helped the Unicorn

Lady to carry the unicorn out on that dreadful day – they asked all three of us to carry it back in again. The flags were flying, the band was playing. Everyone was cheering and clapping. Mother and Grandma were there too. They both cried, I noticed, and I loved that. The Mayor made a speech which began: "This is the Day of the Unicorn, the greatest day our town has known, the day we can all make a new start together." There were fireworks that evening, and singing and dancing. It was the proudest, happiest day of my life.

Now, all these years later, we have peace again in our country. We were lucky. Unlike other towns we did not lose too many people. Only Ivan Zec, the postman, didn't come home again after the war. He died in a prison camp somewhere. And Frano's brother, Tonio came back blind, with one leg missing. So all is not the same again. The truth is that after war nothing is ever the same again. But the Unicorn Lady still works in the town library, still reads her stories to the children after school. I do it too, from time to time, when she asks me to, because I'm a writer now, a weaver of tales. And if from time to time I lose the thread of my story, I just go and sit on the magical unicorn in the library, and my story flows again.

So I believe in unicorns.
I believe in them absolutely.

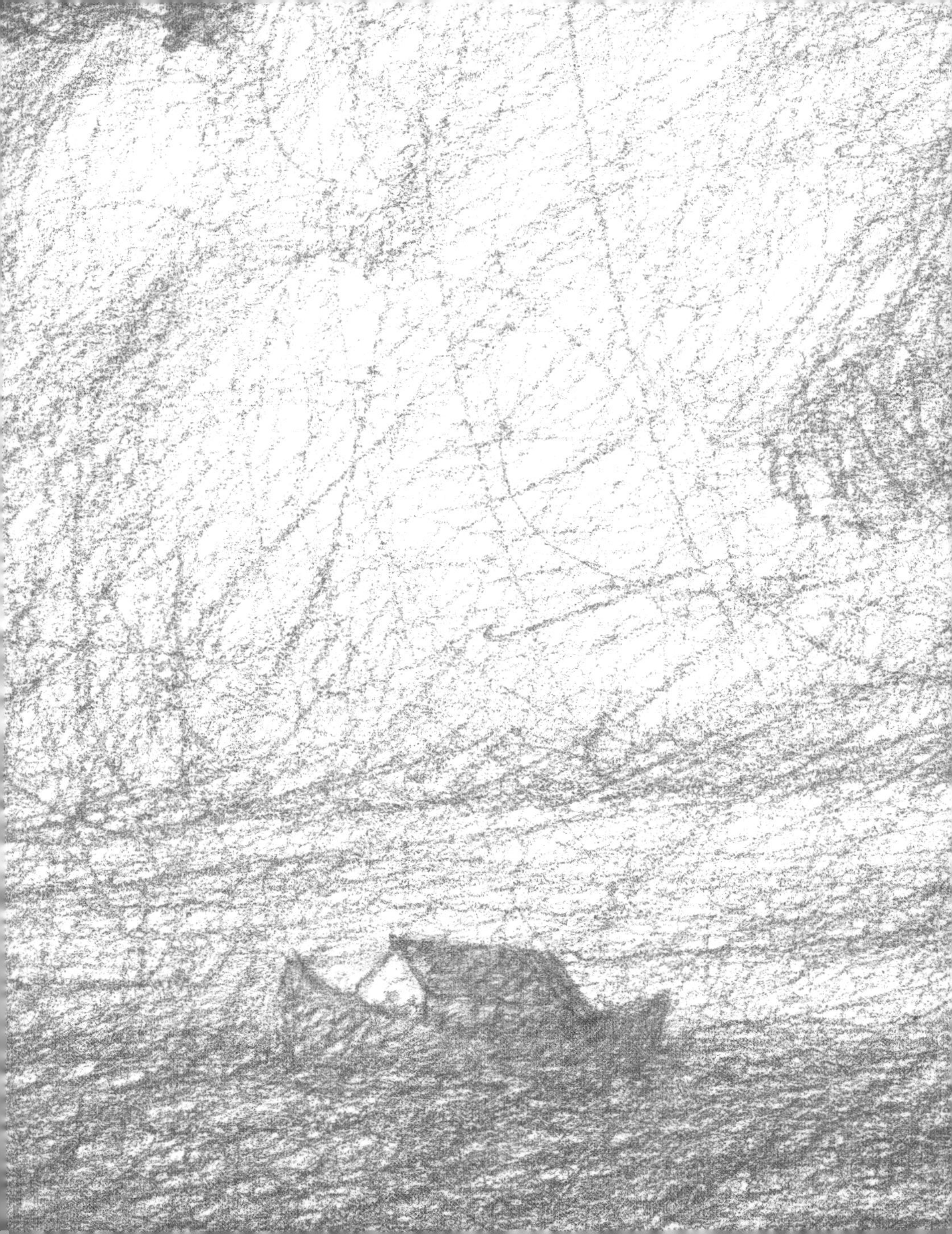

The

kites

are

flying!

This edition published 2010 by Walker Books Ltd, 87 Vauxhall Walk, London SE11 5HJ • 10 9 8 7 6 5 4 3 2 1 • Text © 2009 Michael Morpurgo • Illustrations © 2009 Laura Carlin • The right of Michael Morpurgo and Laura Carlin to be identified as author and illustrator respectively of this work has been asserted by them in accordance with the Copyright, Designs and Patents Act 1988 • This book has been typeset in Gill Sans • Printed in China • All rights reserved. No part of this book may be reproduced, transmitted or stored in an information retrieval system in any form or by any means, graphic, electronic or mechanical, including photocopying, taping and recording, without prior written permission from the publisher. • British Library Cataloguing in Publication Data: a catalogue record for this book is available from the British Library • ISBN 978-1-4063-2603-1 • www.walker.co.uk

For the children who live on both sides of the wall, who will one day bring it tumbling down. No guns or trumpets needed. MM
For Maia, Molly and Smudge. LC

The kites
are flying!

Michael
Morpurgo

illustrated by

Laura Carlin

WALKER
BOOKS

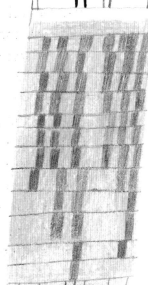

Ist May 2008
Nearly midnight. Gruesome hotel. Jerusalem airport.

Wish I wasn't here. Sometimes I really do wonder why I write a diary at all. It's useful enough I suppose when I'm actually filming – helps me to remember details I might forget, the sequence of events, and so on. But on nights like this I know I'm doing it just out of habit. I've written in my diary every day since I can remember. I can see the point of it after the truly memorable days, but then I would probably remember those anyway. The truth is that there have been so many days I just want to forget. Days like today.

Traffic jams all the way to the airport. Late arriving. Ages checking in. Plane delayed anyway, so I needn't have expended all that fury and frustration. Can't those security people at least try to smile while they're rifling through your bag? I mean, what's their problem? Then we had to fly into the most violent turbulence I've ever known. I should be used to it by now – I do enough flying. But this time I really did think my number was up. Some of the lockers flew open, and the lady next to me started saying her prayers.

We didn't land at Jerusalem. We bumped. Bumpity, bump-ity, bump. It was as if the pilot was reverting to his child-hood. The plane was a stone he was skimming across a lake. On and on it went, and we were inside it. Then there were more unsmiling security people. Late into this ghastly air-port hotel where I know I'm not going to sleep. The sheets and towels stink of chemicals. The only air I can breathe is noisy, because I can't switch off the air-conditioning.

When I phoned home for a bit of comfort, Penny said everything was fine. She sounded a bit sleepy, but she said I hadn't woken her up. Jamie had been a bit hyper appar-ently when he came home from school, but he was fast asleep now. She'd read him his King Arthur book, again. She told me that Jamie said I read it better than she did. She was a bit miffed about that. But I wasn't. It made me smile, probably my first smile all day. Makes a fellow feel better to smile. Penny told me she missed me, that she wished I could be at home, and then we wouldn't have to be phoning each other in the middle of the night. "Max, do you realize what time it is?" she said. She wasn't cross ex-actly, but I could tell she didn't want to talk much after that. I felt very alone after she put the phone down. Still do.

Mustn't get gloomy. Got to sleep. Can't be gloomy if you're asleep. Early start tomorrow. Must find out about the buses first thing. The food on the plane was disgusting. I only ate it because it was there, which was pretty stupid. And now I've got bellyache.

Hey, Mahmoud, are you there? Are you

there? Can you hear me? I had my beautiful dream again last night, the same dream, about the kites. Uncle Yasser says it is a foolish dream. But it isn't foolish, is it, Mahmoud?

You're always telling me not to listen to old Uncle Gasbag. It's your dream, that's what you say. You dream what you want to dream, little brother. I like it when you call me little brother. You know something? You're not only my big brother, you're my best friend. Hey, I saw that girl again, the one in the blue headscarf. She was there again today, waving to me, and she was in my dream too. She was waving to me then as well. She does it every time!

Mahmoud, are you listening? I'm afraid to close my eyes in case I have that nightmare again. You told me the nightmares would go away when the dream comes true. What was it you said? 'You only dream the beautiful dream, little brother, because of the nightmare. It's like day always follows night. You can't have the one without the other. Light is only light,' you said, 'when you've seen how dark the dark is'. I still don't understand that, Mahmoud. There's a lot you tell me I don't really understand. But I don't mind.

I like it when you talk to me. I like it so much. Will you fly
my kite with me tomorrow? Will you be there under the
kite tree?

It's the same every time I have to go to bed. I want to
go on talking to you all night long, Mahmoud. I suppose I
shouldn't talk to you as much as I do – you must get fed up
with me – but there's no one else I can talk to, no one else
I want to talk to either, no one else who knows, no one
else who was there. You are my big brother, 12 years old
– that's four years older than me – and I tell you everything.
I'm always thinking about you, even when I'm not talking to
you. I'm so proud of you – the fastest runner in the whole
village! But you're more than just my big brother, you've

12

been the father of the family too, since Father was taken away by the occupiers and put in a prison camp back when I was little. We haven't seen him since. So you have had to help out on the farm with Uncle Yasser, Uncle Gasbag.

Everything you have ever planted grows well – Uncle Yasser says it's your green fingers. Broad beans, aubergines, sunflowers, olives, lemons – they all grow. But you have always liked the sheep best of all, sitting on the hillside all day long, looking after the sheep. You know all of them, and they know you. They love you and they trust you. It's like you're their big brother too. I like being out there with you and the sheep, Mahmoud. I like feeling the warm wind on my face, and smelling the wild thyme. We lie there watching

13

the hawks hovering on the wind. We talk, we laugh, we dream. You are a dreamer too, like me. I think we even dream the same dreams.

But we don't lie out there on the hillside just dreaming. We make our kites, and we fly them. When I hold the spool and let out the string, you race out over the hillside, whooping and yelling as the kite catches the wind. Then it's up there, and flying high. You make the kite swoop and soar, again and again. Sometimes it crashes into a tree, or dives into the hillside. You are always angry with yourself then, and

won't speak to me. But after a while, when you've calmed down, I tell you that maybe we should just mend it, or make another one, and we do. Each one we make is better than before – different, bigger, smaller, with a longer tail maybe, or a shorter one. They're all painted different colours too, some like birds, some like butterflies, some even like fish. On summer evenings the whole village comes out to watch us. They stand there, gazing up into the sky and loving our kites as much as we do. It's the only time we can forget all our troubles and sadnesses, and just be happy again, for a while anyway.

You remember that afternoon, Mahmoud, when I asked you why kites seem to make everyone so happy, why people laugh out loud when they see them soaring up there in the sky. I remember every word you told me, Mahmoud, as if it was yesterday. But it wasn't yesterday, it was two years ago next week.

'Every time I fly a kite, little brother, I'm thinking it's me up there, and that I'm far away from all this down here, far away from the soldiers and the checkpoints and the tanks. Up there I'm out of it. I go wherever the wind takes me, and no one can stop me. No soldiers, no checkpoints, no tanks,' you said.

And then you were angry, Mahmoud. Whenever you

16

talked about the occupiers you always got angry. And that
time you cried, Mahmoud. You cried because you were
so angry. 'Why do they keep Father in prison, Said?' you
asked me. 'Tell me that, Said. Why do they come here and
take our lands? Why do they treat us like donkey muck?
Why can't they just go home and leave us in peace?' Then
you told me about the soldier. 'I want to tell you something, Said', you said. 'It happened yesterday. I can't stop
thinking about it. I saw this soldier. He was down at the
checkpoint, and I was coming across the road driving the
sheep. He was looking straight down the barrel of his
rifle into my eyes. Then I saw his face under the helmet.
I couldn't believe it, he didn't look any older than me.

I'm thinking, You're someone's son too. I'm thinking, one day you're going to kill me maybe, and you won't even know why you're doing it. Do you know what I did then? I smiled at him. I didn't want to look frightened, so I smiled at him, just to show him. He smiled back, I promise you he did, even gave me a wink. So then I'm thinking that they can't be all bad, these occupiers. There's the girl in the blue headscarf who waves to me over the wall sometimes, and this soldier. That's two. So if they're not all bad, and we're not all bad, why can't the good ones on both sides just get together and sort it all out? Then the soldiers could all go home, and Father could be let out of prison and come home to us, and everything would be right again.' There were tears running down your cheeks and I remember you brushed them away with the back of your hand. 'I miss Father, Said,' you said. 'Sometimes I miss him so much that it hurts.'

You know the honest truth, Mahmoud? I hardly remember Father. He's been gone so long. I know him mostly from those photos Mother shows me. But I don't like looking at them, because Mother always cries when she talks about him, and I hate it when she does that. When she cries it's like my whole head is filling up with tears, like it's bursting with sadness. I like it much better when you tell me about Father, because you've told me so many funny stories about him. I love it when I'm sitting under the kite tree and thinking about the things you told me about him, how Father taught you everything you know: how to make kites, how to plant broad beans, how to whistle the sheep in, how to play football. I remember I told you once you were rubbish at football, and you wrestled me onto my back and sat on top of me, threatening to tickle me to death unless I took it back. So I took it back. 'Anyway, little brother, do you think anyone at Barcelona or Manchester United makes better kites than me?' That's what you said. Then you tickled me half to death, and we rolled over and over, screeching and giggling. We looked up and there were all the sheep staring at us as if we were completely mad, which made us laugh all the more. We laugh a lot, don't we, Mahmoud? I love to hear you laugh.

Mahmoud? Are you there? I was thinking about you again this afternoon, under the kite tree. It's a good place for thinking. But I talk to you best when I'm in bed at night, don't I? I don't know why. Maybe it's because it's more secret. But the kite tree's my favourite place in the whole world. I love that old tree. Uncle Gasbag says it's the oldest tree on the hillside, at least ten grandfathers old. That's why it's all twisted and crooked, just like he is. It's the best shade on the whole farm, so the sheep love it too. We've put a lot of kites together under that tree, haven't we? It's our kite tree, yours and mine, Mahmoud. That's why it's the place I most love to be, because you're always there. And that's where I was this afternoon, when I first saw him.

I could see someone walking along the road down in the valley. He'd just got off the bus. I knew right away he wasn't one of us. None of us would wear a hat like that. And I knew he wasn't an occupier from the settlement on the other side of the wall. They don't wear hats like that either. He kept stopping every now and again to look around him, as if it was all new to him, as if he was a stranger.

Then he saw me, saw the sheep, and the kite tree. He turned off the road and began climbing up the hillside towards me. He had a rucksack on his back, and that silly hat on his head, and he had some kind of equipment slung over his shoulder. And I'm thinking, He's one of those television reporters, that's what he is. We see them coming through the village often enough, don't we? But usually they're in Land Rovers, and usually there's lots of them. But this one was alone, and on foot. And I thought, I don't want him to come any closer. He's going to disturb the sheep, I know he is. They're already getting up and moving away. They don't like strangers any more than I do. Best to stay where I am and ignore him. I'll get on with my kite and hope he'll just go away. But then I thought that maybe, before he goes away, I might get some chocolate off him. Television people are always fair game for chocolate, and sometimes dollars too, if you're lucky. I know how it works: if you want to get lucky with these reporter guys, then you have to smile at them, and do it as if you mean it. You have to call them 'Mister' too – you told me that, Mahmoud, remember? I can't call him 'Mister', but I can look up at him and smile.

When I did, I saw he was just a few steps away from me, taking off his silly hat, and wiping his brow with the back of his hand. He was all puffed out from the climb. He took off his rucksack, and put all his equipment down on the ground right beside me.

I'm telling you, Mahmoud. He's got the coolest camera I've ever seen in all my life! I didn't want chocolates any more. I didn't even want dollars. I just wanted to hold that camera. I wanted to make a movie with it. I love movies. You love movies too, don't you, Mahmoud. ET, Shrek. I liked Shrek 2 best. The donkey – I love that donkey.

Are you there, Mahmoud? Are you there?

2nd May

Roof of village house
(don't yet know the name
of the village, will find out tomorrow) West Bank. 11.10 p.m.

Now I know why I make films. I need reminding sometimes, and today has reminded me. It's to capture moments, great moments, so that they are held for ever on film, so that one fleeting day does not simply merge into the next fleeting day, and become part of the blur of existence. I feel tonight as if I'm really living inside a story, that I'm a part of it. I'm no longer merely reporting on it. I'm not sure this has ever happened to me quite like this before.

I have the night sky starry above me, and I'm writing by torchlight. These are the same stars that were shining over 2,000 years ago, on the first Christmas night. That was the picture of this land that I grew up with as a child – it was a place of shepherds and angels and stables and stars. Of course I've learnt since that the Holy Land wasn't at peace then, and it most certainly isn't now. The images are all too familiar: the bombed-out buses, the tanks and soldiers in the streets, the stone-throwing children, the masked gun-men marching, the hilltop settlements, the squalor of the refugee camps, the funerals, the burials, the grief. But I'm here for the wall. It's the wall more than anything that has haunted me. It's the wall that has brought me here.

It all depends on how old you are. For some people it is the television footage of the assassination of President Kennedy, or the pictures of Neil Armstrong stepping down onto the surface of the moon. For others it might be Nelson Mandela walking out of prison in South Africa, or it might be those planes slamming into the Twin Towers of Manhattan. For most of us there is a happening we have witnessed at an impressionable time of our lives that we shall never for-get. For me as a youngster, it was sitting on the floor with a bunch of college friends, watching in utter astonishment as the Berlin Wall came tumbling down in front of our eyes.

It was the day when people decided enough was enough, and they wanted to be free. They climbed up onto the wall, and began to pull it down with their bare hands, this wall that had divided the world for so long, and had brought us to the brink of nuclear war. To see that wall coming down was the single most hopeful, most momentous time of my young life. I wrote about it in my diary, copiously, pages and pages of it, rambling stuff when I read it now, romantic, rapturously optimistic. But I was young then.

Now another wall has been built – nothing new about walls, of course, Hadrian's Wall, the Great Wall of China, and plenty of others. But this one is now, and, like the Berlin Wall, the passions it arouses threaten once more to engulf the world in global conflict. I had to come to see it for myself. I want to make a film, tell the story, but from both sides of the wall, Palestinian, then Israeli.

I want to find out how it is to live in the shadow of this wall, to tell a story that does not point the finger, that does not accuse, but tells it as it is. That was my plan, and it still is. But today, the first day of filming, hasn't worked out at all as I'd imagined it would. The totally unexpected has happened.

I've discovered over the years that if you travel by bus or train, you get close to people, get to talk to them if you're lucky. Cars isolate you. So I've been travelling on buses for most of the day. Lots of dust, lots of checkpoints, some filming as I went, but not too much – I didn't want to attract attention. I did the last leg of my journey up to this village on foot, and that was when I came across the shepherd boy.

It was late afternoon. He was sitting alone on the hillside under an ancient olive tree with a gnarled and spiralling trunk. He had his sheep all around him. Until that moment I had seen nothing even remotely picturesque in this tragic land, little that reminded me in any way of its Biblical past. All I'd seen were newly built hilltop settlements, green valleys below, and scattered across the landscape as far as the eye could see, small, straggling stone-built villages. And everywhere, there was the wall, snaking its way around the hills, a symbol of oppression and occupation for one side, a protective defensive partition for the other.

The shepherd boy at once made me forget all that. He was making a kite, and was clearly so intent upon it that he did not even notice me coming. He was whistling softly as I came climbing up the hill towards him, not so much to make a tune, I thought, as to reassure his sheep. When he did look up at me, he showed no surprise or alarm. He looked about the same age as Jamie, perhaps a little older, and had the same sort of smile too, open-hearted and engaging. I felt I couldn't wander on past him with just a wave, or a meaningless nod of the head. And anyway, I needed a rest after my long and exhausting trudge up the hill. So I stopped, sat down under the tree and offered him a drink out of my rucksack. He shook his head at first, but when I pressed him he took the bottle and drank eagerly. When he handed the bottle back, he said nothing. He wasn't talkative, but he wasn't sullen either. When I told him my name, he didn't seem to want to tell me his. I could see then that he wasn't a bit interested in me anyway.

It was my video camera. He couldn't take his eyes off my video camera. It's a new one, the latest Sony, digital, state-of-the-art technology, light, neat, beautifully designed and made; the best I've ever worked with. The shepherd boy seemed in awe of it, completely fascinated. I thought that maybe this was the way we might make some kind of contact, a way to get talking, through my video camera. It seemed like a good idea.

When I offered to let him hold it, his whole face lit up. But I could tell pretty soon that just holding it wasn't going to be enough. So I showed him all the functions, how to work everything. He never spoke a word, but I knew he was taking everything in. Soon he was making it quite clear that he wanted to have a go with it. Having gone this far, I could hardly refuse. We walked out from under the tree, looking for something to film. Almost at once he was pointing up into the sky. There was a hawk hovering there, so I let him film it. Afterwards he wanted to film the sheep, then me in my hat. He liked my hat a lot, I could tell that. But he did not even try to speak to me, and I thought that was strange. We sat down under the tree again, and watched the replay of his film. He insisted on seeing it over and over again.

I wanted to get him to talk, so I tried to explain to him as best I could, that this was what I did, that I was a cameraman, and that I had come to make a film about the wall. It was obvious he didn't understand a word I was saying. I kept on trying. But whether I spoke in English or in the few words of Arabic I know made no difference. His smile was the only response I got. He just didn't seem to want to talk, yet I had the distinct impression that he wanted me to go on talking. And I certainly got the feeling that he was quite happy for me to stay. Or maybe it was just that he wanted my camera to stay. He still could hardly keep his eyes off it.

I could see talking wasn't getting me anywhere. So I decided I would get on and do what I had come here for. I got to my feet, picked up the camera, and indicated that I wanted to film him – him and his sheep. "Do you mind?" I asked him. "Is it alright?" Still he wouldn't speak. He just smiled and shrugged, and I wasn't sure whether this meant yes or no. I didn't want to risk upsetting him. So I sat down again, and we lapsed into silence, the sheep gathering all around us again under the shade of the olive tree, their smell pungent and heavy in the warm air. When the shepherd boy began to work on his kite again, I thought maybe I had outstayed my welcome. But then, quite suddenly, he reached across, picked up my camera and handed it to me. Permission granted! I knew then, that this boy must understand a whole lot more than his silence lets on.

I began with a wide-angle shot of the shepherd boy under the tree, with the kite on his lap, his sheep all around him, and the wall in the distance. None of it was any use though, because he would keep looking up at the camera and smiling, and holding up his half-made kite to show me. He put my hat on his head, and began to mimick me filming him. He was good, too. I recognized my body language instantly. But it was pointless to go on filming. We shared what food we had. He took a great fancy to my chocolate digestive biscuits – Jamie's going-away present to me – and he gave me some pinenuts out of his pocket. We shared our silence too. It was the best we could manage, and maybe after all, I thought, as good a way as any to get to know one another. I showed him the photo I keep in my wallet of Penny and Jamie and me in the garden at home in London. He liked that. He looked at it intently for a very long time before he gave it back. Then, with evening coming on, he stood up and began to whistle his sheep home. I thought it was time for me to set off on my way too.

I followed him, the sheep clambering around me, bleating at me. It was a steep climb, and very soon I was finding it hard to keep up. Ahead of me the boy was springing from

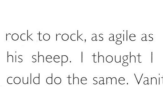

rock to rock, as agile as his sheep. I thought I could do the same. Vanity, vanity. Where he could leap, I could leap. No problem. Wrong. I landed awkwardly, felt my ankle twist under me, and found myself sitting there in amongst the rocks, clutching my ankle, moaning and cursing all at the same time. The shepherd boy came running back. He got me to my feet, and put his arm around me to support me. I hobbled with him all the way up into the village. His arm was strong around me, stronger than I'd have thought possible for a boy of his size.

Half an hour or so later I found myself sitting in the boy's home, my ankle throbbing less now in a bowl of cold water, and surrounded by his large extended family, all talking to each other – about me I was sure – and watching me, if not with open hostility, then certainly with some suspicion. They were polite, but wary. The boy, I noticed, still did not speak, even amongst his own family. He was proudly showing them the progress he'd made on his kite that day. I could see he was a much treasured child.

We ate lamb, and the most succulent broad beans I've ever tasted, and sweetly spiced cake, dripping with honey. Luckily, there were still enough of my chocolate digestive biscuits to share around, so I could make some contribution, at least, to the feast. When the boy came and sat himself down beside me, I sensed he was doing so because he wanted to make it very clear to everyone, including me, that I was his special guest. I felt honoured by that, and moved by his affection. But soon enough it dawned on me that he had another reason for sitting himself down next to me. He began tapping my arm and pointing at my camera. He wanted to hold it again, to demonstrate to his family that he knew precisely how it worked. He still didn't speak, not a word. He just showed them. He put on my hat, and made believe he was me. He was the cameraman, turning the camera on each of them, and last of all on me too. Then he was going into a whole performance, acting out how I'd fallen over in the rocks. There I was clutching my ankle and rolling about in agony, rocking back and forth, then hobbling back home, leaning on him. He had everyone in fits by now, me too.

Later he came fishing in my pocket for my wallet. He found the photo and passed it all around, so that everyone in the family could have a good look. It was this, as much as all his showing off and playacting, that broke down some of their reserve towards me. I think the boy knew they would look at me differently once they'd seen the photo. That's why he did it, I'm sure.

The boy used almost exactly the same method of postponing bedtime as Jamie. His delaying tactics are only different in one respect: he goes about it entirely silently. Jamie's protests are infinitely noisier. But they share the same absolute determination not to go to bed. The boy was appealing directly to his mother, yet at the same time pleading his case to everyone, that he needed more time to finish his kite. He did this skilfully, wordlessly, making it quite clear to all of us what it was that still needed to be done, and that it was really unfair to expect him to go to bed until it was finished. All he needed was just a little more time to finish it. The mistake he made was that in the end he did finish it. He was still protesting as his mother hustled him off to bed, leaving me alone with his family.

Once he'd gone there followed a long and awkward silence. After a time I decided it was up to me to try to end it. I thought the best way of doing this might be to venture a word or two in Arabic.

"A fine boy," I said – that's what I thought I'd said anyway, that's what I hoped I'd said. There were smiles all around. I must have said the right thing, in more or less the right way. But the silver-bearded man on my left was still suspicious of me. I took him to be the head of the family. He certainly looked the oldest, and he seemed to be the one to whom everyone else deferred. When he spoke to me it was in quite good English, and with very little hesitation.

"I am Yasser Hussein. I am Said's uncle. I wish to say that you are welcome in our home. You have been kind to Said, and for this we are grateful. As you say, he is a fine boy, but he is a troubled boy."

"He is very quiet," I said. "He does not say very much. My son Jamie, back at home, he's the noisy kind." The old man translated what I'd said for the others. The whole room seemed suddenly filled with sadness. He turned back to me, looking me full in the eye now. It was a searching gaze, and very disconcerting, but I returned it as best I could. It was an uncomfortably long while before he spoke again.

"You are a television reporter?"

"Yes."

"Whose side are you on? Theirs or ours?"

"I'm on no one's side." Still that same penetrating look.

"But you are Said's true friend?"

"Yes."

"Then maybe there is something you should know. Said cannot tell you this himself, because he cannot speak. Not any more. There was a time, not so long ago, when he was, as you say your son is, noisy, very noisy. And like Mahmoud, Said speaks good English too, better than me. They learn it at school, but more from films on the television, I think. I tell you, you could not stop Said from talking."

"I don't understand," I said.

"None of us understand," he told me. "None of us will ever understand. All we know is that it was God's will. And it must be God's will also that you come here to our house. It is good you come here, because you make Said smile and laugh. Your camera makes him smile. Your hat

40

makes him laugh. We like to see this. It is good for him to be happy again. We hope always for the best for Said, we pray for it. We are all very proud of him. Maybe he does not speak, but he is the best shepherd boy in all of Palestine. He knows all of the sheep by name, every one of them, just like Mahmoud. And like Mahmoud he makes the best kites in all of Palestine too. But Said's kites are not ordinary kites, you know, not like anyone else's kites."

"What do you mean?" I asked him.

"Maybe he will show you that himself," he told me. "Maybe he will fly his kite for you tomorrow. This one is almost ready to fly, I think. But for Said the wind must be perfect. The wind must be always from the east, and not too strong, or Said will not fly his kites."

He got up then, and when he did, everyone did. He was still unsmiling as he said goodnight. I felt I had passed a kind of test, but an important one. The evening was over.

My ankle still feels a bit tender. It's swollen too, but I don't think it's as bad as I thought it was. I can wriggle my toes. Hurt like hell when it happened, but nothing is broken. Just a sprain. I can't put much weight on it. They've given me a stick. I can manage, just about. I have to. There's no way I'm going to miss going out with Said and his sheep tomorrow. I just hope the wind is right, and that he does fly his kite. That's something I have to be there to film. I know now that it isn't just me that Said doesn't speak to. He can't speak at all. Or he won't. I want to know why. Why can't he speak? And who is this Mahmoud that Said's Uncle Yasser was on about? There are so many things I've got to find out about. Tomorrow. Tomorrow.

Hey, Mahmoud. Are you listening?

Are you there? It's dark. I don't want to sleep. I want to talk to you.

This man, Mahmoud, he's not like any of the other television reporters who've been to the village before. I will tell you about this man, Mahmoud. Alright, so he's a bit clumsy on his feet, but his chocolate biscuits must be the best in the whole world. And he's kind too. He let us have all of them, enough for everyone in the family, and he didn't even have one himself. That's not all. I mean, you have to check out his video camera! Smartest camera you've ever seen. Sony, digital, and he let me use it! I got to hold it myself, and he showed me how to work it. And, and, and … he let me make a real film, all on my own. Sort of on my own, anyway. The hawk came flying over the kite tree, hovering there just like he does every evening, and Mister Max taught me how to hold the camera tight and steady, how to zoom in on him close and hold the shot. You know something, Mahmoud? When I was looking through the lens I was so close to that hawk that I could see every one of his wing feathers trembling in the wind. I'm not kidding.

43

It was like he was near enough for me just to reach out and touch him. And Mister Max has got a son back home. He looks a bit like you, Mahmoud. Got a big nose, and lots of teeth when he smiles. I've seen a photo.

Anyway, Mister Max went and tripped over, which was very funny, but he's done in his ankle, which is why he's been sitting down there with his foot in that bowl of water. Like I told you, he's a bit clumsy. I brought him home. I had to. Couldn't leave him there, could I? You should've seen Uncle Gasbag's face when he saw us. You know what he's like, hates all reporters, says he doesn't trust them. What am I doing bringing one of his kind into our home? Don't I know they're all liars, all on the side of the occupiers? But Mother likes Mister Max because he likes her honey cake, and the others all like him too on account of the film he let me make … and because of the chocolate biscuits. Even Uncle Yasser liked the camera. You know what I think? I think that sometimes Uncle Gasbag just pretends to be a grumpy old goat. He's fixing up a crutch for Mister Max, for tomorrow, so I think he liked him really.

Hey, Mahmoud. You should have seen Mister Max eating his honey cake. He licked his fingers afterwards, just like you.

Only without the loud slurping noise that always makes me laugh. So I laughed at Mister Max too, and then everyone laughed, even Uncle Yasser. Mahmoud, I think this has been the happiest day for a long time, since you … since it happened. Mahmoud? Are you still there, Mahmoud?

I want to tell you about something else. It's the kite I'm making. I'm having trouble with it. It's the glue again. The paper keeps coming away from the frame. I've mixed the glue properly, just like you taught me. Alright, I might have hurried it a bit. I can hear you telling me, 'Don't hurry it, Said. You always hurry things. Take your time. A kite will fly when it's ready to fly, in its own good time. It's like a living thing. It's not just paper and wood and string.' I want to fly it tomorrow, Mahmoud. It's important. I want to show Mister Max how beautiful it is. I want the wind to be right. I want the girl in the blue headscarf to be there too. I won't fly it unless she's there. I never do. And I won't forget to wave to her for you, I promise.

I won't sleep. I know I won't. I've got too many thoughts whirling round and round in my head. I don't mind. I don't want to sleep anyway. I don't want to live through the nightmare. If I stay awake I won't have the nightmare.

I'll stay awake. I'll talk to myself. That'll do it.

Everyone in the family thinks that flying the kites is a waste of time, except you of course. But it isn't. And in the village they all know what I'm doing, and why I'm doing it too. They shake their heads at me; they feel sorry for me. At school, they just think I'm mad. They don't say so, not out loud. But that's because of you, Mahmoud, because they don't want to be unkind to your little brother. I see it in their eyes though. Sometimes it really gets me down. I know, you've told me before, you're always telling me, I've got to keep going, because it's the right dream to have, the right thing to do, the only way to work things out.

But there are some things you won't tell me, however much I ask. I want you to tell me why it had to happen like it did, why it had to be you, why the kite had to crash-land down in the valley that morning. Uncle Gasbag always says it was God's will. Oh, and that's supposed to make it alright, is it, Uncle? It wasn't God who was flying the kite, was it? It was me. I was the one who crashed it. I was the one who was moaning on and on about how it wasn't fair that you flew the kites more than I did, how I only got to hold the spool and let out the string. If you hadn't given in to me like you did, if you hadn't let me fly the kite, none of it would have happened. If you'd been flying the kite yourself, you'd have controlled it better, kept it flying, I know you would. You wouldn't have panicked like I did, and the kite wouldn't have crashed down by the road. It probably wouldn't have crashed at all. You know how to fly kites better than anyone else in the whole village, in the whole world, Mahmoud, everyone knows that. You should have been flying it, not me. Then it wouldn't have happened, and you wouldn't have had to go running down the hill to pick it up. And if you hadn't gone there...

3rd May

10.30 p.m. Addulah Village. Same rooftop. Another starry, starry night.

Ankle's a lot better, thanks to the crutch. Wouldn't have been able to manage at all today without that. Still don't know which of them arranged it for me. It appeared from nowhere. I just found it beside me when I woke up. They're kind, these people, wonderfully kind. Long day. Good day. Important day. But it's been a sad day too. I'm tired. Hobbling about like Long John Silver all day has been exhausting, but I think maybe I might be making the most extraordinary film I've ever made. Difficult to remember everything that's happened, but I'll try. It's been a day I never want to forget.

I was up before dawn and went, alone, down into the valley. I needed to film the sun coming up over the wall. I wanted to capture a whole day in this place, sunrise to sunset. After I'd filmed the dawn, I climbed back up the hill, so that I could get a long shot of the wall from just below the village – I had to have the villagers' constant view of it.

I tracked it up through the olive groves and over the hillside to the settlement beyond where the flag flies. The more I look at it, the more I want to see the wall from their side too. Do they feel just as imprisoned over there by the wall as these people do? I have to find out. Dogs barked at one another from both sides, cocks crowed, donkeys brayed.

After breakfast I went off with Said and his sheep, Said carrying some of my equipment as well as his kite, now with string and spool attached. That was when I first saw there was some writing in Arabic on one side of the kite, but I didn't know what it meant, and I couldn't ask him. I doubted he'd be flying his kite that day anyway, because there wasn't a breath of wind.

A couple of hours later though, as I was sitting under the kite tree with the sheep browsing in amongst the rocks, I felt a sudden wind spring up. Said was on his feet at once. He ran out onto the open hillside, and stood there for a while, his head lifted into the wind. I was filming him sur-reptitiously from under the tree. I think he knew I was, but by now he was paying no attention at all to me, nor to the camera. Clearly he had something much more important on his mind. Then I saw him turn and wave at me, frantically.

50

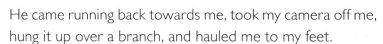

He came running back towards me, took my camera off me, hung it up over a branch, and hauled me to my feet.

He thrust the spool into my hands, showed me what to do, and went racing out over the hill with the kite. I watched him holding it high, letting it go, saw the wind take it and fly it. I marvelled at the beauty of it, wondered at the exhilaration on his face. But it was only when he took the spool from me, handed me the string and let me fly it, that I felt that same joy for myself. The kite was wind-whipped and soaring above us, tugging to be free, longing to go higher, and Said was jumping up and down in wild delight as it swooped and hovered overhead. It was an old joy I had almost forgotten. I had done it like this with my father when I was a boy – I had tried it with Jamie a few times, but there was never enough wind, or maybe we just weren't very good at it. This was supreme. The kite was alive at the end of the string, loving it as much as I was. But all too soon, Said was tugging at my arm. He wanted the string back. I was just getting the hang of it, and wasn't at all happy about giving it up. But I had no choice.

Said was a real expert. With a tweak of his wrist the kite turned and twirled. With a flick of his fingers he dived it and danced it. It was mesmerizing. But after a while I remembered

what I was there for, and my professional instinct kicked in. I had to have boy and kite in the same shot, so I needed to put some distance between them and me. I picked up my camera and began to film. I did not want to miss such an idyllic image. I closed on the fluttering kite, tracked its flight until the wall was there in the background. I tightened on the wall and tracked it up over the hillside, then zoomed in on the settlement beyond, on the blue and white flag flying there.

That was when I noticed there were some children in the street below, kicking a football about. When one of them scored, I could see there were the usual recriminations on one team, and all the over the top celebrations on the other. Same the world over, I was thinking. When I turned my camera on Said again, I saw there was a frown of intense concentration on his face. I don't know how, but I think I knew what he was about to do, so when it happened it didn't really surprise me. He just let the kite go. It was quite deliberate. He simply gave it to the wind, holding his arms up as if he was releasing a trapped bird and giving it its freedom. The kite soared up high, floating there on the thermals before the wind discovered it and took it away over the olive grove, over the wall and up towards the hilltop settlement beyond.

I felt Said tugging insistently at my sleeve. He was trying to get the camera off me. He wasn't just wanting to have another go at filming. There was an urgency in his eyes. So I gave him the camera. He was looking through the lens across at the settlement. I saw at once what he was focussing on. There was a girl in a wheelchair. She was gazing up at the kite as it came floating down. When it landed, she wheeled herself over and picked it up. She was wearing a blue headscarf. For a few moments she sat there looking across at us, the kite on her lap, shielding her eyes against the sun, as the footballers came racing over towards her. They stood there then, all of them gazing across the wall at us. Said handed me back the camera, and then he was waving both his hands in the air. Only the girl waved back, flourishing the kite above her head. The footballers were all drifting away by now. The two went on waving to one another for several minutes, long enough for me to film it. They didn't seem to want to stop.

On the way back home to the village that evening with the sheep we came across Uncle Yasser harvesting his broad beans. I stopped and asked if he'd mind if I filmed him at his work. He shrugged. "There is not much to film," he told me. "It's a poor crop, but it's always a poor crop. There's never enough water, that's the trouble. They have taken most of it. And they have taken all our best land for themselves. They leave us only the dust to farm in. So what can you do?" He was watching Said as he walked on up into the village with his sheep. "I see he has sent his kite away. He let it go. The wind must have been just right. He never keeps his kites, not one of them. He just makes another one, waits for the next east wind, and then sends it off again. Did you see what he writes on his kites? 'Salaam.' This means Peace. And on every one of them he writes both their names, 'Mahmoud and Said'." I had not expected him to want to talk so willingly.

"How many has he sent?" I asked him.

"We are not sure. And he cannot tell us of course. Maybe about one a week since Mahmoud … and that was nearly two years ago now."

I felt I could ask, because I felt he wanted to tell me. "Who is this Mahmoud? What happened?" He gave me a long and hard look. I thought I had gone too far then, intruded too much. I stopped filming, because I thought that was what he wanted.

"No," he said gravely. "You must film this. I want the world to hear about Mahmoud, about how he lived and how he died. You are Said's friend. I think he trusts you. I think he would want you to know. Only Said knows what happened. He was there. He saw it with his own eyes." I was filming him again by the time he went on.

"Mahmoud was Said's older brother. He loved to make kites. He loved to fly kites, and always with Said. It happened two years ago next week, next Monday – before the occupiers built the wall. I knew there would be trouble that day, we all did. A settler's car was ambushed that morning, further down the valley. We heard that a woman was killed, and her daughter was in hospital with bad injuries to her legs, that maybe she would die too. So we said to all the children in the village: this is a dangerous time, you must stay inside, everyone is safer inside if the soldiers come. But Mahmoud, like his father, was a strong-willed boy, and he became angry with me when I said he could not go out with the sheep and fly his kite. He told me the sheep had to go out, that he would fly his kite whenever and wherever he

wanted, that they had put his father in prison, that he would not let them make a prisoner of him in his own home, that he would not hide away like a coward. These were the last words Mahmoud spoke to me.

"And so they went off, the two of them together, with the sheep. Whenever Mahmoud went out, Said would always want to go with him. His mother tried to stop them too. They wouldn't listen.

"Maybe an hour later, we heard a helicopter come flying low over the village. There was some shooting. When it was over we all ran outside. We saw Mahmoud lying at the bottom of the hill, beside the road. Said was with him, Mahmoud's head on his lap. When we got there, his eyes were open, but he was dead. We asked Said how it happened. But he cannot tell us. Since that moment, he has not spoken. God willing, one day he will. God willing."

His voice was breaking. He looked away from me, trying to compose himself. I was doing much the same thing. I couldn't bring myself to ask him any more questions. But when he turned to me again, I could see he was ready to tell me more.

"Said sent off his first kite the next day, the day we buried Mahmoud. Do you know why he sends his kites over there? He cannot tell us himself of course, but we think that for Said every kite that lands over there in the settlement is like a seed of friendship. This is why he writes 'Salaam' on each one. We think that he hopes and he believes that one day they'll send the kites back, and everything will be right, that his father will come home from prison, that somehow friendships will grow, all the killing will stop, and peace will come. For Said, his kites are kites of peace. You know what I think? I think, let Said have his dreams. It's all he has. He'll find out soon enough what they're like over there. Many people tell him this. Uncle Gasbag I may be, but I know when a thing must not be spoken. Let him dream, I say, let him dream."

"But what about the girl?" I asked him. "The one with the blue headscarf, the one in the wheelchair. She picked up Said's kite. She waved at him. I saw her. She was trying to be friendly. It's a beginning, surely."

He wasn't having any of it. "I have seen this girl. We all have," he said. "She's alive, isn't she? It is Mahmoud who is dead, is it not? Tell me, what does it cost to wave? They cannot wave away what they did. She is an occupier, isn't she? They are all occupiers. All occupiers are the same."

I spent the evening here in the family house, on my knees on the floor with Said, helping him make his new kite, everyone looking on. He caught my eye from time to time. I think there is so much he wants to tell me that he cannot tell me. I see in his eyes someone who believes completely in his dream, and I know he wants me to believe in it too.

I want to, but I'm finding that very hard. I think he can sense my doubt. I hope he can't.

I should have phoned home today, and now it's too late. Anyway, I'm too sad to talk, and it would all be too difficult to explain how things are here over the phone. Tomorrow, I'll talk to them tomorrow. One thing I've decided I have to do. When I film the wall from the other side, that has to be the settlement I go to. I have to go to where Said's sending his kites. I'm going to try to meet up with that girl in the wheelchair, to talk to those kids playing football. I have to see and hear the whole story, to know it as it's lived on both sides. Everything's as silent as the stars up here, and as beautiful as peace. Time to sleep. G'night Jamie. G'night Penny.

Hey, Mahmoud?

Are you there, Mahmoud? Are you listening? I waved to the girl, Mahmoud, and she waved back too. That's 94 of our kites she's got now. Mahmoud? Mahmoud? You will stay with me, won't you? I don't want to go to sleep. I don't want the nightmare again. I want to stay awake and talk to you. Don't leave me. You know how I hate the dark. I've got so much to tell you.

I flew the kite with Mister Max today. He was hopeless. He was making a real mess of it, and I didn't want him to crash it. So I took it off him in the end, and showed him how to do it. You should've seen me. It went so high. I mean, out of sight … well, almost. You won't want to hear this, but I'm as good at flying kites as you … well, almost. Anyway I'm a whole lot better at it than Mister Max, that's for sure. He's alright on the spool. I just have to nod and he lets out a little bit more. He's a bit slow. The last time I flew a kite with anyone else, it was with you, Mahmoud. It was that day, Mahmoud. Remember? Oh, Mahmoud, I don't want to remember, I don't want to, but I can't stop myself. It's my nightmare again, like a black hole waiting for me and

63

I'm falling. I'm falling into it. Mahmoud! Mahmoud! Help me!

I'm flying the kite, and I'm loving it. You're on the spool, and you're going on and on about how Uncle Gasbag tried to keep us indoors, about how this was our hillside, and how no one could stop us flying our kites, not Uncle Yasser, not the soldiers, not the tanks, not anyone. I'm only half listening to you, because I'm trying to concentrate on the kite. I'm doing well too, diving it as fast as you, so fast I can hear the rush and the roar of it in the wind as it whizzes by over our heads. And I'm laughing, laughing to see it up there, looping and swooping. I'm still laughing when the roaring of the kite becomes a thunder and a throbbing in my ears. I'm so frightened because the ground underneath me is shaking, and I can't understand why, until I see the helicopter coming up over the hilltop behind us, and close, so close, almost touching the top of the kite tree. The sheep are going crazy, Mahmoud.

You're angry, Mahmoud. You're yelling at the helicopter, picking up a stone and throwing it, then another stone and another. The helicopter's right over us, and we're being blown away by it, and I'm losing all control of the kite.

It's spiralling crazily away down towards the road and it's crashing into the rocks. You're yelling at me to stay where I am, and then I see you racing down the hill after it. I've got my hands over my ears and I'm crying because I know already that something terrible is going to happen. I see the tank coming round the bend in the road before you do, and I'm screaming at you, Mahmoud, trying to warn you, but you can't hear me.

You're crouching over the kite now, and then you look up and see the tank. I know what you're going to do, and I know that there's nothing I can do to stop you. You're too angry. 'Mahmoud! Mahmoud! Don't do it!' But you do it. You run at the tank, shouting and screaming at it, hurling

stones at it. When they open fire you still don't stop. You only stop when you fall, and when you fall you're lying still, so still.

The soldiers tell me it's a mistake. They were firing warning shots, they say. They are sorry, they say. One of the soldiers is crying, but I'm not going to cry any more, not in front of them. There's blood. There's so much blood. You are trying to tell me something. 'Mend the kite, Said. Can you hear me? Mend the kite.'

Yes, I can hear you. I'll mend the kite. Then I'll make another and another. I promise. I promise.

I'm still promising when the light goes out of your eyes, Mahmoud. You're looking at me and you're not seeing me.

• • •

But you are not dead, Mahmoud. I won't let you be dead. You will never be dead for me. I can hear your voice in my head. I know you're there when I talk to you. And you're in every one of the kites I make. When they fly, you fly. When you fly, you're alive. You're flying high, looking down at me, waiting for the right wind, for the right moment to make the dream happen. I wish it would happen soon. I know it will, but I want it to be soon. I want Mister Max to see it with his own eyes. He doesn't believe it now, but he will then. He'll have to, won't he? The girl in the blue headscarf believes it, I know that. Don't ask me how. I just know she does. She's there every day, sitting outside in her wheelchair watching me fly the kites. She's waiting for the moment. She's the girl you used to wave to. She wasn't in a wheelchair then, only afterwards. So it must be her, the girl who was injured in the ambush that day down on the road, the one whose mother was killed. She has binoculars. I can see the sunlight flashing on them some-times. I'm sure she knows who I am too, that I'm your little brother. If I know who she is, then why shouldn't she know who I am?

I think it must be her father who wheels her out into the sun every day, checks the brakes on the wheelchair and leaves her there. Sometimes it must be her brother, who comes with them, and who goes off to play football with his friends. But she doesn't watch the football. She watches me, and my kites, and I watch her. We wave to each other too whenever I send over a kite. In the last few months she's been wheeling herself about more and more, so I think she's getting stronger each day. We sit and look at one another over the wall; me from under the kite tree, her from the field below the settlement. There's something strange happening between us, Mahmoud. The more we look across at one another, the more our thoughts seem to fly to each other over the wall. When I'm thinking of you, Mahmoud, I know she's thinking of you too. It's weird, I know, but I really can feel what she's thinking sometimes. And weirder still, I know she knows what I'm thinking too. She knows my dream. Sometimes I think maybe it was her dream before it was ever my dream. Perhaps we made it together. All I know for sure is that we dream the same dream. Don't ask me how.

• • •

Hey, Mahmoud, I want to tell Mister Max all about my dream and the girl in the wheelchair. I so wish I could speak again. I want to tell him all about you, Mahmoud, and the soldier who cried when he saw what he'd done. He would tell it truthfully to the world on the television, and then everyone would know what happened that day to you. Maybe if people really understood what bullets do, then it would stop. He'll be going soon, tomorrow he says, if his ankle's better. I hope it's not better. I want him to stay. I shall miss him when he's gone, him and his camera. But I'm making myself a promise, Mahmoud. I am deciding right now that when I grow up I shall make films like he does. I've worked it out. If I can't talk, then I'll tell our story in pictures, the story of you, Mahmoud, of our village, all about our kites, and the wall and the settlement, and the girl in the blue headscarf who waves to us. I shall tell everyone about our nightmare and our dream, and about how one day we'll make it come true. It is my story, and the girl's story. Together we will make it come true.

Now I'm going to sleep. No more nightmares, only dreams. Goodnight, Mahmoud. Goodnight.

4th May

On a bus to visit the settlement. West Bank. 6.30 p.m.

After all that happened today, I have never wanted to meet anyone so much as that girl in the blue headscarf. So that's where I'm headed now, to talk to her, to find out her story. It's a bumpy old ride, but I have to try to write this down now, whilst it's still fresh in my head. Think about it any longer, and I might persuade myself that none of it happened, that it was just a dream.

When I woke up this morning I could feel my ankle was a lot better, a lot stronger. There was still a weakness there, but most of the pain had gone. So I didn't need the crutch any more, just a stick. I said my goodbyes to the family after breakfast. I shall come back and see them again when the film's done and dusted. I want to show it to them. I want them to see I've been truthful, that I've told the story as it is, as it happened. The language has

been a barrier, and I know my film will be the poorer for it. Without Uncle Yasser there to interpret, I felt awkward and inadequate sometimes. But I never once felt awkward with Said.

The whole family was there to see me off when I left the village this morning with Said and the sheep. As we went down the hill, Said's hand slipped into mine, and I knew it wasn't just to help me over the rocks. There was the same unspoken thought between us. We were friends, good friends. I didn't want to leave, and he didn't want me to go. The sheep were in a clambering mood, their bleating and their bells noisy around us as we walked. We sat down together under the old olive tree. Said had brought the frame of his new kite with him, but he wasn't in the mood for working on it. He seemed lost in sadness. He was looking out over the valley, over the wall to the settlement beyond. A donkey brayed balefully from somewhere nearby, winding itself up into a frenzy of misery. I decided it was better to get the parting over with quickly. I put my hand on his shoulder, and let it rest there for a few moments. We were both too upset to say any other kind of goodbye. I got up, gathered up my rucksack and my equipment, and left him sitting there.

When I looked back a while later I saw that Said was busy with his kite. I decided to stop and to film him, the perfect closing shot, just what I needed. I was just about organized and ready to film, when Said sprang to his feet. The sheep were bounding away from him, scattering all over the hillside.

Then I saw the kites. The sky above the settlement was full of them, dozens of them, all colours and shapes, a kaleidoscope of kites. Like butterflies they danced and whirled around each other as they rose into the air. I could hear shrieks of joy, all coming from the other side of the wall. I saw the crowd of children gathered there, every one of them flying a kite. Some of the kites snagged each other and spiralled down to earth, but most sailed up magnificently, skywards. The settlers were running out of their houses to watch. Then, one after the other the kites were released, and left to the wind, and on the wind they flew out over the wall towards us.

From behind us now, from Said's village, the people came

running too, as the kites began to land in amongst us, and amongst the terrified sheep too. Uncle Yasser picked up one of them. "You see what they wrote? 'Shalom'," he said. "It says 'Shalom'. Can you believe that? And look, look!" On the other side of the kite they had drawn a dove. We soon discovered there was the same message, and the same drawing, on all of them.

Everywhere, on both sides of the wall, children were cheering and laughing, and leaping up and down. I could see the girl in the wheelchair was struggling to stand up. When at last she made it, with the help of a couple of her friends, she took off her scarf and waved it wildly over her head.

All around me, Said's family, and many of the other villagers, mothers and fathers, grandmothers and grand-fathers, began to clap, hesitantly at first. Soon everyone was joining in, Uncle Yasser too. But I noticed then that it was only the children who were whooping and whistling and laughing. The hillsides rang with their jubilation, with their exultation. It seemed to me like a glorious symphony of hope.

I had to be with Said at his moment of triumph. I stumbled as fast as I could back towards him, and as I came closer I could hear him laughing and shouting out loud, along with all the other children. I realized then, idiot that I was, that I had quite forgotten to film this miracle. But almost simultaneously I understood that it didn't matter anyway, that it was the laughter that mattered. It was laughter that would one day resonate so loud that this wall, like all the others, would come tumbling down. No trumpets needed, as they had been once at Jericho, only the laughter of children.

And then Said was running up to me, and taking me by the hands. "Mister Max, are you seeing it? The girl, she is sending back the kites. I knew she would do it. I knew it. It's her dream, it's my dream, it's our dream. But it's not a dream any more is it? It's a real happening, isn't it? Are you hearing me, Mister Max? It's me, me speaking my voice, isn't it?" He put his head back, closed his eyes, and shouted out loud to the sky above. "Hey, Mahmoud! Mahmoud! Can you hear me? Can you see this? The kites are flying, Mahmoud! The kites are flying!"

Afterword by Jeremy Bowen

Palestinian children like Said and Mahmoud really do fly kites. On hot afternoons in the West Bank a perfect kite-flying breeze blows out of the desert into the hills. In Gaza it comes in off the sea. Just like Said and Mahmoud, the children make their own kites, out of newspapers, old plastic bags and bits of wood. They turn what sounds like a pile of rubbish into something beautiful.

For the best part of a century Arabs and Jews have been fighting over this small piece of land that lies between the river Jordan and the Mediterranean Sea. The conflict often sends shockwaves around the world.

Many children have been wounded and killed. The pain that families on both sides feel when it happens is just the same. In my work as a reporter I have been to many funerals, and to homes full of sadness, where there are children who have seen brothers, sisters or parents killed.

My job is to help people understand why the conflict exists and why it doesn't stop. Sometimes that means trying to show what it is like to be a person caught up in it, at the very worst time of their lives. And sometimes, though not often enough, we find a few signs of hope too.

Homecoming

For Emma and Rupert M.M.
For Oscar, Felix, Osian and Inigo P.B.

This is a work of fiction. Names, characters, places and incidents are
either the product of the author's imagination or, if real, are used
fictitiously. First published 2006 as "Singing for Mrs Pettigrew"
in *Singing for Mrs Pettigrew: A Story-maker's Journey* by
Walker Books Ltd, 87 Vauxhall Walk, London SE11 5HJ
This edition published 2012 as *Homecoming* • 10 9 8 7 6 5 4 3 2 1
Text © 2006 Michael Morpurgo • Illustrations © 2012 Peter Bailey
The right of Michael Morpurgo and Peter Bailey to be identified
as author and illustrator respectively of this work has been asserted
by them in accordance with the Copyright, Designs and Patents
Act 1988 • This book has been typeset in Bembo • Printed in China
All rights reserved. No part of this book may be reproduced,
transmitted or stored in an information retrieval system in any
form or by any means, graphic, electronic or mechanical, including
photocopying, taping and recording, without prior written
permission from the publisher. • British Library Cataloguing in
Publication Data: a catalogue record for this book is available from
the British Library • ISBN 978-1-4063-4107-2 • www.walker.co.uk

Homecoming

Michael Morpurgo

illustrated by

Peter Bailey

**WALKER
BOOKS**

I was near by anyway, so I had every excuse to do it, to ignore the old adage and do something I'd been thinking of doing for many years. "Never go back. Never go back." Those warning words kept repeating themselves in my head as I turned right at the crossroads outside Tillingham and began to walk the few miles along the road back to my childhood home in Bradwell, a place I'd last seen nearly fifty years before. I'd thought of it since, and often. I'd been there in my dreams, seen it so clearly in my mind, but of course I had always remembered it as it had been then.

Fifty years would have changed things a great deal, I knew that. But that was part of the reason for my going back that day, to discover how intact was the landscape of my memories.

I wondered if any of the people I had known then might still be there; the three Stebbing sisters perhaps, who lived together in the big house with honeysuckle over the porch, very proper people so Mother always wanted me to be on my best behaviour. It was no more than a stone's throw from the sea and there always seemed to be a gull perched on their chimney pot. I remembered how I'd fallen ignominiously into their goldfish pond and had to be dragged out and dried off by the stove in the kitchen with everyone looking askance at me, and my mother so ashamed. Would I meet Bennie, the village thug who had knocked me off my bike once because I stupidly wouldn't let him have one of my precious lemon sherbets? Would he still be living there? Would we recognize one another if we met?

The whole silly confrontation came back to me as I walked. If I'd had the wit to surrender just one lemon sherbet he probably wouldn't have pushed me, and I wouldn't have fallen into a bramble hedge and had to sit there humiliated and helpless as he collected up my entire bagful of scattered lemon sherbets, shook them triumphantly in my face, and then swaggered off with his cronies, all of them scoffing at me, and scoffing my sweets too. I touched my cheek then as I remembered the huge thorn I had found sticking into it, the point protruding inside my mouth. I could almost feel it again with my tongue, taste the blood. A lot would never have happened if I'd handed over a lemon sherbet that day.

That was when I thought of Mrs Pettigrew and her railway carriage and her dogs and her donkey, and the whole extraordinary story came flooding back crisp and clear, every detail of it, from the moment she found me sitting in the ditch holding my bleeding face and crying my heart out.

She helped me up onto my feet. She would take me to her home. "It isn't far," she said. "I call it Dusit. It is a Thai word which means 'halfway to heaven'." She had been a nurse in Thailand, she said, a long time ago when she was younger. She'd soon have that nasty thorn out. She'd soon stop it hurting. And she did.

The more I walked the more vivid it all became: the people, the faces, the whole life of the place where I'd grown up. Everyone in Bradwell seemed to me to have had a very particular character and reputation, unsurprising in a small village, I suppose: Colonel Burton with his clipped white moustache, who had a wife called Valerie, if I remembered right, with black pencilled eyebrows that gave her the look of someone permanently outraged – which she usually was. Neither the colonel nor his wife was to be argued with. They ruled the roost. They would shout at you if you dropped sweet papers in the village street or rode your bike on the pavement.

Mrs Parsons, whose voice chimed like the bell in her shop when you opened the door, liked to talk a lot. She was a gossip, Mother said, but she was always very kind. She would often drop an extra lemon sherbet into your paper bag after she had poured your quarter pound from the big glass jar on the counter. I had once thought of stealing that jar, of snatching it and running off out of the shop, making my getaway like a bank robber in the films. But I knew the police would come after me in their shiny black cars with their bells ringing, and then I'd have to go to prison and Mother would be cross. So I never did steal Mrs Parsons' lemon sherbet jar.

Then there was Mad Jack, as we called him, who clipped hedges and dug ditches and swept the village street. We'd often see him sitting on the churchyard wall by the mounting block eating his lunch. He'd be humming and swinging his legs. Mother said he'd been fine before he went off to the war, but he'd come back with some shrapnel from a shell in his head and never been right since, and we shouldn't call him Mad Jack, but we did. I'm ashamed to say we baited him sometimes too, perching alongside him on the wall, mimicking his humming and swinging our legs in time with his.

But Mrs Pettigrew remained a mystery to everyone. This was partly because she lived some distance from the village and was inclined to keep herself to herself. She only came into the village to go to church on Sundays, and then she'd sit at the back, always on her own. I used to sing in the church choir, mostly because Mother made me, but I did like dressing up in the black cassock and white surplice and we did have a choir outing once a year to the cinema in Southminster – that's where I first saw *Snow White* and *Bambi* and *Reach for the Sky*. I liked swinging the incense too, and sometimes I got to carry the cross, which made me feel very holy and very important.

I'd caught Mrs Pettigrew's eye once or twice as we processed by, but I'd always looked away. I'd never spoken to her. She smiled at people, but she rarely spoke to anyone; so no one spoke to her – not that I ever saw anyway. But there were reasons for this.

Mrs Pettigrew was different. For a start she didn't live in a house at all. She lived in a railway carriage, down by the sea wall with the great wide marsh all around her. Everyone called it Mrs Pettigrew's Marsh. I could see it best when I rode my bicycle along the sea wall. The railway carriage was painted brown and cream and the word PULLMAN was printed in big letters all along both sides above the windows. There were wooden steps up to the front door at one end, and a chimney at the other. The carriage was surrounded by trees and gardens, so I could only catch occasional glimpses of her and her dogs and her donkey, bees and hens. Tiny under her wide hat, she could often be seen planting out in her vegetable garden, or digging the dyke that ran around the garden like a moat, collecting honey from her beehives perhaps or feeding her hens. She was always outside somewhere, always busy. She walked or stood or sat very upright, I noticed, very neatly, and there was a serenity about her that made her unlike anyone else, and ageless too.

But she was different in another way. Mrs Pettigrew was not like the rest of us to look at, because Mrs Pettigrew was "foreign", from somewhere near China, I had been told. She did not dress like anyone else either. Apart from the wide-brimmed hat, she always wore a long black dress buttoned to the neck. And everything about her, her face and her hands, her feet, everything was tidy and tiny and trim, even her voice. She spoke softly to me as she helped me to my feet

that day, every word precisely articulated. She had no noticeable accent at all, but spoke English far too well, too meticulously, to have come from England.

So we walked side by side, her arm round me, a soothing silence between us, until we turned off the road onto the track that led across the marsh towards the sea wall in the distance. I could see smoke rising straight into the sky from the chimney of the railway carriage.

"There we are: Dusit," she said. "And look who is coming out to greet us."

Three greyhounds were bounding towards us followed by a donkey trotting purposefully but slowly behind them, wheezing at us rather than braying. Then they were gambolling all about us, and nudging us for attention. They were big and bustling, but I wasn't afraid because they had nothing in their eyes but welcome.

"I call the dogs Fast, Faster and Fastest," she told me.

"But the donkey doesn't like names. She thinks names are for silly creatures like people and dogs who can't recognize one another without them. So I call her simply Donkey." Mrs Pettigrew lowered her voice to a whisper. "She can't bray properly – tries all the time but she can't. She's very sensitive too; takes offence very easily." Mrs Pettigrew took me up the steps into her railway carriage home. "Sit down there by the window, in the light, so I can make your face better."

I was so distracted and absorbed by all I saw about me that I felt no pain as she cleaned my face, not even when she pulled out the thorn. She held it out to show me. It was truly a monster of a thorn. "The biggest and nastiest I have ever seen," she said, smiling at me. Without her hat on she was scarcely taller than I was. She made me wash out my mouth and bathed the hole in my cheek with antiseptic. Then she gave me some tea which tasted very strange but warmed me to the roots of my hair. "Jasmine tea,"

she said. "It is very healing, I find, very comforting. My sister sends it to me from Thailand."

The carriage was as neat and tidy as she was: a simple sitting room at the far end with just a couple of wicker chairs and a small table by the stove. And behind a half-drawn curtain I glimpsed a bed very low on the ground. There was no clutter, no pictures, no hangings, only a shelf of books that ran all the way round the carriage from end to end. From where I was sitting I could see out over the garden, then through the trees to the open marsh beyond.

"Do you like my house, Michael?" She did not give me time to reply. "I read many books, as you see," she said. I was wondering how it was that she knew my name, when she told me. "I see you in the village sometimes, don't I? You're in the choir, aren't you?" She leant forward. "And I expect you're wondering why Mrs Pettigrew lives in a railway carriage."

"Yes," I said.

The dogs had come in by now and were settling down at our feet, their eyes never leaving her, not for a moment, as if they were waiting for an old story they knew and loved.

"Then I'll tell you, shall I?" she began. "It was because we met on a train, Arthur and I – not this one, you understand, but one very much like it. We were in Thailand. I was returning from my grandmother's house to the city where I lived. Arthur was a botanist. He was travelling through Thailand collecting plants and studying them. He painted them and wrote books about them. He wrote three books; I have them all up there on my shelf. I will show you one day – would you like that? I never knew about plants until I met him, nor insects, nor all the wild creatures and birds around us, nor the stars in the sky. Arthur showed me all these things. He opened my eyes. For me it was all so exciting and new. He had such a knowledge of this wonderful world we live in, such a love for it too. He gave me that, and he gave me much more: he gave me his love too.

"Soon after we were married he brought me here to England on a great ship – this ship had three big funnels and a dance band – and he made me so happy. He said to me one day on board that ship, 'Mrs Pettigrew' – he always liked to call me this – 'Mrs Pettigrew, I want to live with you down on the marsh where I grew up as a boy.' The marsh was part of his father's farm, you see. 'It is a wild and wonderful place,' he told me, 'where on calm days you can hear the sea breathing gently beyond the sea wall, or on stormy days roaring like a dragon, where larks rise and sing on warm summer afternoons, where stars cascade on August nights.'

"'But where shall we live?' I asked him.

"'I have already thought of that, Mrs Pettigrew,' he said. 'Because we first met on a train, I shall buy a fine railway carriage for us to live in, a carriage fit for a princess. And all around it we shall make a perfect paradise and we shall live as we were meant to live, amongst our fellow creatures, as close to them as we can be. And we shall be happy there.'

"So we were, Michael. So we were. But only for seventeen short months, until one day there was an accident. We had a generator to make our electricity; Arthur was repairing it when the accident happened. He was very young. That was nearly twenty years ago now. I have been here ever since and I shall always be here. It is just as Arthur told me: a perfect paradise."

Donkey came in just then, clomping up the steps into the railway carriage, her ears going this way and that.

She must have felt she was being ignored or ostracized, probably both. Mrs Pettigrew shooed her out, but not before there was a terrific kerfuffle of wheezing and growling, of tumbling chairs and crashing crockery.

When I got home I told Mother everything that had happened. She took me to the doctor at once for a tetanus injection, which hurt much more than the thorn had, then put me to bed and went out – to sort out Bennie, she said. I told her not to, told her it would only make things worse. But she wouldn't listen. When she came back she brought me a bag of lemon sherbets. Bennie, she told me, had been marched down to Mrs Parsons' shop by his father and my mother, and they had made him buy me a bag of lemon sherbets with his own pocket money to replace the ones he'd pinched off me.

Mother had also cycled out to see Mrs Pettigrew to thank her. From that day on the two of them became the best of friends, which was wonderful for me because I was allowed to go cycling out to see Mrs Pettigrew as often as I liked. Sometimes Mother came with me, but mostly I went alone. I preferred it on my own.

I rode Donkey all over the marsh. She needed no halter, no reins. She went where she wanted and I went with her, followed always by Fast, Faster and Fastest, who would chase rabbits and hares wherever

they found them. I was always muddled as to which dog was which, because they all ran unbelievably fast – standing start to full throttle in a few seconds. They rarely caught anything but they loved the chase.

With Mrs Pettigrew I learnt how to puff the bees to sleep before taking out the honeycomb. I collected eggs warm from the hens, dug up potatoes, pulled carrots, bottled plums and damsons in Kilner jars. (Ever since, whenever I see the blush on a plum I always think of Mrs Pettigrew.) And always Mrs Pettigrew would send me home afterwards with a present for Mother and me, a pot of honey perhaps or some sweetcorn from her garden.

Sometimes Mrs Pettigrew would take me along the sea wall all the way to St Peter's Chapel and back, the oldest chapel in England, she said. Once we stopped to watch a lark rising and rising, singing and singing so high in the blue we could see it no more. But the singing went on, and she said, "I remember a time – we were standing almost on this very same spot – when Arthur and I heard a lark singing just like that. I have never forgotten his words. 'I think it's singing for you,' he said, 'singing for Mrs Pettigrew.'"

Then there was the night in August when Mother and Mrs Pettigrew and I lay out on the grass in the garden gazing up at the shooting stars cascading across the sky above us, just as she had with Arthur, she said. How I wondered at the glory of it, and the sheer immensity of the universe. I was so glad then that Bennie had pushed me off my bike that day, so glad I had met Mrs Pettigrew, so glad I was alive. But soon after came the rumours and the meetings and the anger, and all the gladness was suddenly gone.

I don't remember how I heard about it first. It could have been in the playground at school, or Mother might have told me or even Mrs Pettigrew. It could have been Mrs Parsons in the shop. It doesn't matter. One way or another, everyone in the village and for miles around got to hear about it. Soon it was all anyone talked about. I didn't really understand

what it meant to start with. It was that first meeting in the village hall that brought it home to me. There were pictures and plans of a giant building pinned up on the wall for everyone to see. There was a model of it too, with the marsh all around and the sea wall running along behind it, and the blue sea beyond with models of fishing boats and yachts sailing by. That, I think, was when I truly began to comprehend the implication of what was going on, of what was actually being proposed. The men in suits sitting behind the table on the platform that evening made it quite clear.

They wanted to build a power station, but not just an ordinary power station, a huge newfangled atomic power station, the most modern design in the whole world, they said. They had decided to build it out on the marsh – and everyone knew by now they meant Mrs Pettigrew's Marsh. It was the best place, they said.

It was the safest place, they said, far enough outside the village and far enough away from London. I didn't understand then who the men in suits were, of course, but I did understand what they were telling us: that this atomic power station was necessary because it would provide cheaper electricity for all of us; that London, which was only fifty or so miles away, was growing fast and needed more electricity. Bradwell had been chosen because it was the perfect site, near the sea so the water could be used for cooling, and near to London, but not too near.

"If it's for Londoners, and if it's so safe, what's wrong with it being right in London then?" the colonel asked.

"They've got water there too, haven't they?" said Miss Blackwell, my teacher.

Mrs Parsons stood up then, beside herself with fury.

"Well, I think they want to build it out here miles away from London because it might blow up like that bomb in Hiroshima. That's what I think. I think it's wicked, wicked. And anyway, what about Mrs Pettigrew? She lives out there on the marsh. Where's she going to live?"

Beside me Mother was holding Mrs Pettigrew's hand and patting it as the argument raged on. There'd be any number of new jobs, said one side. There are plenty of jobs anyway, said the other side. It would be a great concrete monstrosity; it would blight the whole landscape. It would be well screened by trees, well landscaped; you'd hardly notice it; and anyway you'd get used to it soon enough once it was there. It would be clean too, no chimneys, no smoke. But what if there was an accident, if the radiation leaked out? What then?

Suddenly Mrs Pettigrew was on her feet. Maybe it was because she didn't speak for a while that everyone fell silent around her. When she did speak at last, her voice trembled. It trembled because she was trembling, her knuckles bone-white as she clutched Mother's hand. I can still remember what she said, almost word for word.

"Since I first heard about this I have read many

books. From these books I have learnt many important things. At the heart of an atomic power station there is a radioactive core. The energy this makes produces electricity. But this energy has to be used and controlled with very great care. Any mistake or any accident could cause this radioactive core to become unstable. This could lead to an explosion, which would be catastrophic, or there could be a leak of radiation into the atmosphere. Either of these would cause the greatest destruction to all forms of life, human beings, animals, birds, sea life and plants, for miles and miles around. But I am sure those who wish to build this power station have thought of all this and will make it as safe as possible. I am sure those who will operate it will be careful. But Arthur, my late husband, was careful too. He installed a simple generator for our home. He thought it was safe, but it killed him.

"So I ask you, gentlemen, to think again. Machines are not perfect. Science is not perfect. Mistakes can easily be made. Accidents can happen. I am sure you understand this. And there is something else I would like you to understand. For me the place where you would build your atomic power station is home. You may have decided it is an uninteresting place and unimportant, just home to one strange lady who lives there on the marsh with her donkey and her dogs and her hens. But it is not uninteresting and it is not unimportant. It is not just my home either, but home also for curlews and gulls and wild geese and teal and redshanks and barn owls and kestrels. There are herons, and larks. The otter lives here and the fox comes to visit, the badger too, even sometimes the deer. And amongst the marsh grass and reeds and the bulrushes live a thousand different insects, and a thousand different plants.

"My home is their home too and you have no right to destroy it. Arthur called the marsh a perfect paradise. But if you build your atomic power station there, then this paradise will be destroyed for ever. You will make a hell of paradise."

Her voice gained ever greater strength as she spoke. Never before or since have I heard anyone speak with greater conviction.

"And I do mean for ever," she went on. "Do not imagine that in fifty years, or a hundred maybe, when this power station will have served its purpose, when they find a new and better way to make electricity — which I am quite sure they will — do not imagine that they will be able to knock it down and clear it away and the marsh will be once again as it is now. From my books I know that no building as poisonous with radiation as this will be will ever be knocked down. To stop the poison leaking it will, I promise you, have to be enclosed in a tomb of concrete for hundreds of years to come. This they do not want to tell you, but it is true, believe me. Do not, I beg you, let them build this power station. Let us keep this marsh as it is. Let us keep our perfect paradise."

As she sat down there was a ripple of applause which swiftly became tumultuous. And as the hall rang loud with cheering and whistling and stamping I joined in more enthusiastically than any. At that moment I felt the entire village was united in defiance behind her. But the applause ended, as – all too soon – did both the defiance and the unity.

The decision to build or not to build seemed to take for ever: more public meetings, endless campaigning for and against; but right from the start it was clear to me that those for it were always in the ascendant. Mother stood firm alongside Mrs Pettigrew, so did the colonel and Mrs Parsons; but Miss Blackwell soon changed sides, as did lots of others. The arguments became ever more bitter. People who had been perfectly friendly until now would not even speak to one another. At school Bennie led an ever growing gang who would storm about at playtime punching their fists in the air and chanting slogans. "Down with the Pettigrew weeds!" they cried. "Down with the Pettigrew

50

weeds!" To my shame I slunk away and avoided them all I could.

But in the face of this angry opposition Mother did not flinch and neither did Mrs Pettigrew. They sat side by side at every meeting, stood outside the village hall in the rain with their ever dwindling band of supporters, holding up their placards. SAY NO TO THE POWER STATION they read. Sometimes after school I stood there with her, but when people began to swear at us out of their car windows as they passed by, Mother said I had to stay away. I wasn't sorry. It was boring to stand there, and cold too, in spite of the warmth of the brazier.

And I was always terrified whenever Bennie saw me there, because I knew I'd be his special target in the playground the next day.

Eventually there were just the two of them left, Mother and Mrs Pettigrew. Mad Jack would join them sometimes, because he liked the company and he liked warming his hands over the brazier too. Things became even nastier towards the end. I came out of the house one morning to find red paint daubed on our front door and on our Bramley apple tree, the one I used to climb; and someone – I always thought it must have been Bennie – threw a stone through one of Mrs Pettigrew's windows in the middle of the night. Mother and Mrs Pettigrew did what they could to keep one another's spirits up but they could see the way it was going, so it must have been hard.

Then one day it was in the newspapers. The plans

for the atomic power station had been approved. Building would begin in a few months. Mother cried a lot about it at home and I expect Mrs Pettigrew did too, but whenever I saw them together they always tried to be cheerful. Even after Mrs Pettigrew received the order that her beloved marsh was being compulsorily purchased and that she would have to move out, she refused to be downhearted. We'd go over there even more often towards the end to be with her, to help her in her garden with her bees and her hens and her vegetables. She was going to keep the place just as Arthur had liked it, she said, for as long as she possibly could.

Then Donkey died. We arrived one day to find Mrs Pettigrew sitting on the steps of her carriage, Donkey lying near by. We helped her dig the grave. It took hours. When Donkey had been buried we all sat on

the steps in the half-dark, the dogs lying by Donkey's grave. The sea sighed behind the sea wall, perfectly reflecting our spirits. I was lost in sadness.

"There's a time to die," said Mrs Pettigrew. "Perhaps she knew it was her time." I never saw Mrs Pettigrew smile again.

I was there too on the day of the auction. Mrs Pettigrew didn't have much to sell, but a lot of people came along all the same, out of curiosity or even a sense of malicious triumph, perhaps. The carriage had been emptied of everything – I'd carried some of it out myself – so that the whole garden was strewn with all her bits and pieces. It took just a couple of hours for the auctioneer to dispose of everything: all the garden tools, all the furniture, all the crockery, the generator, the stove, the pots and pans, the hens and the hen house and the beehives. She kept only her books and her dogs, and the railway carriage too. Several buyers wanted to make a bid for it, but she refused. She stood stony-faced throughout, Mother at her side, whilst I sat watching everything from the steps of the carriage, the dogs at my feet.

Neither Mother nor I had any idea what she was

about to do. Evening was darkening around us, I remember. Just the three of us were left there. Everyone else had gone. Mother was leading Mrs Pettigrew away, a comforting arm round her, telling her again that she could stay with us in the village as long as she liked, as long as it took to find somewhere else to live. But Mrs Pettigrew didn't appear to be listening at all. Suddenly she stopped, turned and

walked away from us back towards the carriage.

"I won't be long," she said. And when the dogs tried to follow her she told them to sit where they were and stay.

She disappeared inside and I thought she was just saying goodbye to her home, but she wasn't. She came out a few moments later, shutting the door behind her and locking it.

I imagined at first it was the reflection of the last of the setting sun glowing in the windows. Then I saw the flicker of flames and realized what she had done. We stood there together and watched as the carriage caught fire, as it blazed and roared and crackled, the flames running along under the roof, leaping out of the windows, as the sparks flurried and flew. The fire engines came, but too late. The villagers came, but too late. How long we stood there I do not know, but I know that I ached with crying.

Mrs Pettigrew came and lived with us at home for a few months. She hardly spoke in all that time. In the end she left us her dogs and her books to look after and went back to Thailand to live with her sister. We had a few letters from her after that, then a long silence, then the worst possible news from her sister.

Mrs Pettigrew had died, of sadness, of a broken heart, she said.

Mother and I moved out of the village a year or so later, as the power station was being built. I remember the lorries rumbling through, and the Irish labourers who had come to build it sitting on the church wall with Mad Jack and teaching him their songs.

Mother didn't feel it was the same place any more, she told me. She didn't feel it was safe. But I knew she was escaping from sadness. We both were. I didn't mind moving, not one bit.

As I walked into the village I could see now the great grey hulk of the power station across the fields. The village was much as I remembered it, only smarter, more manicured. I made straight for my childhood home. The house looked smaller, prettier, and tidier too, the garden hedge neatly clipped; the garden itself, from what I could see from the road, looked too well groomed, not a nettle in sight. But the Bramley apple tree was still there, still leaning sideways as if it was about to fall over. I thought of

knocking on the door, of asking if I might have a look inside at my old bedroom where I'd slept as a child. But a certain timidity and a growing uneasiness that coming back had not been such a good idea prevented me from doing it. I was beginning to feel that by being there I was tampering with memories, yet now I was there I could not bring myself to leave.

I spoke to a postman emptying the postbox and enquired about some of the people I'd known. He was a good age, in his fifties, I thought, but he knew no one I asked him about. Mad Jack wasn't on his wall. Mrs Parsons' shop was still there but now sold antiques and bric-a-brac. I went to the churchyard and found the graves of the colonel and his wife with the black pencilled eyebrows, but I'd remembered her name wrong. She was Veronica, not Valerie. They had died within six months of each other. I got chatting to the man who had just finished mowing the grass in the graveyard and asked him about the atomic power station and whether people minded living alongside it.

"Course I mind," he replied. He took off his flat cap and wiped his brow with his forearm. "Whoever put that ruddy thing up should be ashamed of themselves. Never worked properly all the time it was going anyway."

"It's not going any more then?" I asked.

"Been shut down, I don't know, maybe eight or nine years," he said, waxing even more vehement. "Out of date. Clapped out. Useless. And do you know what they had to do? They had to wrap the whole place under a blanket of concrete, and it's got to stay there like that for a couple of hundred years at least so's it doesn't leak out and kill the lot of us. Madness, that's what it was, if you ask me. And when you think what it must have been like before they put it up. Miles and miles of wild marshland as far as the eye could see. All gone. Must've been wonderful. Some funny old lady lived out there in a railway carriage. Chinese lady, they say. And she had a donkey. True. I've seen photos of her and some kid sitting on a donkey outside her railway carriage. Last person to live out there, she was. Then they went and kicked her out and built that ugly great wart of a place. And for what? For a few years of electricity that's all been used up and gone. Price of progress, I suppose they'd call it. I call it a crying shame."

I bought a card in the post office and wrote a letter to Mother. I knew she'd love to hear I'd been back to Bradwell. Then I made my way past the Cricketers' Inn and the school, where I stopped to watch the children playing where I'd played; then on towards St Peter's, the old chapel by the sea wall, the favourite haunt of my youth, where Mrs Pettigrew had taken me all those years before, remote and bleak from the outside, and inside filled with quiet and peace. Some new houses had been built along the road since my time. I hurried past trying not to notice them, longing now to leave the village behind me. I felt my memories had been trampled enough.

One house name on a white-painted gate to a new bungalow caught my eye: New Clear View. I saw the joke, but didn't feel like smiling. And beyond the

bungalow, there it was again, the power station, massive now because I was closer, a monstrous complex of buildings rising from the marsh, malign and immovable. It offended my eye. It hurt my heart. I looked away and walked on.

When I reached the chapel, no one was there. I had the place to myself, which was how I had always liked it. After I had been inside, I came out and sat down with my back against the sun-warmed brick and rested. The sea murmured. I remembered again my childhood thoughts, how the Romans had been here, the Saxons, the Normans, and now me. A lark rose then from the grass below the sea wall, rising, rising, singing, singing. I watched it disappear into the blue, still singing, singing for Mrs Pettigrew.

Tomas hates school, hates books and hates libraries. But the stories spun by the Unicorn Lady draw him in, making themselves part of him … and changing the course of his life for ever.

"This book needs to be bought for every library, school and home, to share with as many children as we can, that they might experience its magic for themselves." *The Bookseller*

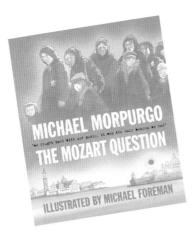

When cub reporter Lesley is sent to Venice to interview a world-renowned violinist, she discovers a long-kept secret – and learns how one group of musicians survived the full horror of war through music.

"Beautifully illustrated, this is a moving tale of secrets, lies and the past." *The Independent*

When young Michael spots a whale on the shores of the Thames, he is sure he must be dreaming. But not only is the creature real … it has a message for him.

"A thought-provoking, touching story with beautiful illustrations on every page."
Primary Times

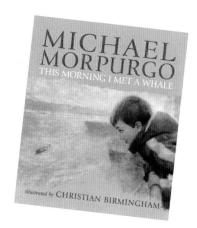

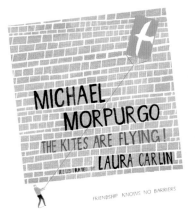

A television reporter's experiences in the West Bank reveal how children's hopes and dreams for peace can fly higher than any wall dividing communities and religions.

"Insightful and beautifully illustrated."
Daily Express

Michael Morpurgo was 2003–2005 Children's Laureate, has written over one hundred books and is the winner of numerous awards, including the Whitbread Children's Book Award, the Smarties Book Prize, the Blue Peter Award and the Red House Children's Book Award. His books are translated and read around the world and his hugely popular novel *War Horse*, already a critically acclaimed stage play, has recently been made into a film. Michael and his wife, Clare, founded the charity Farms for City Children and live in Devon.

Peter Bailey has been illustrating books for over forty years and has worked with many of today's best-known authors, including Dick King-Smith, Allan Ahlberg and Philip Pullman. Of working on *Homecoming,* he says, "I've really enjoyed illustrating this story. It's about time passing and the changes that one sees from childhood to adulthood – and about meeting, early on, someone who influences you for the rest of your life." Peter lives near Liverpool with his wife, Sian, who is also an illustrator.